GOLDTOWN ADVENTURES #2

TUNNEL OF GOLD

SUSAN K. MARLOW

Kregel
Publications

Goldtown Adventures

Badge of Honor
Tunnel of Gold
Canyon of Danger

|||||||||||||||||||||||||||||||||||||||||||||||||||||||||||||||||||||||||||||||||||||||||||||||||||||||||||||||||||||||||||||||||||||||||||||||||||||||||||||||||||||||||||||||||||||||

Tunnel of Gold
© 2013 by Susan K. Marlow

Illustrations © 2013 by Melissa McConnell

Published by Kregel Publications, a division of Kregel, Inc., P.O. Box 2607, Grand Rapids, MI 49501.

ISBN 978-0-8254-4295-7

Printed in the United States of America
13 14 15 16 17 / 5 4 3 2 1

Contents

⤙ CHAPTER 1 ⤚

Delivery Day

GOLDTOWN, CALIFORNIA, 1864

Are you coming or not?" Twelve-year-old Jem Coulter hollered toward the ramshackle ranch house he called home.

There was no answer.

What's taking Nathan so long? Jem frowned at the delay and looked up. The sun was high overhead, the very worst time of day to bounce around in an old wagon, making firewood deliveries. If it were up to Jem, his customers would already have their cooking fuel, and he'd be panning for gold in Cripple Creek with his prospector friend, Strike-it-rich Sam. The sun would still blister his head, but at least his feet would stay cool.

Sweat trickled under Jem's collar, making him itchy. He climbed up on the high wagon seat, unwrapped the reins from around the brake handle, and yelled, "Nathan! Get out here or I'm leaving you behind!"

A faint, "Wait for me!" from inside the house was the only thing that kept Jem from slapping the two horses and taking off without his cousin. He'd promised Nathan a cut of the profits if he helped split, stack, and deliver stove wood this week, but if he didn't hurry up . . .

The screen door creaked open, then slammed shut. A tall, slim boy hurried across the porch, down the steps, and joined Jem at the wagon. "Give me a hand up, would you?"

Jem gaped at him. "Roasted rattlesnakes, Nathan! Did you get your days mixed up? It's not Sunday. Where are you going in that getup?"

He couldn't help but stare. His cousin was dressed in knee-length britches, thick black stockings, and polished shoes. A white shirt and black tie peeked out from inside his dark suit coat. On his blond head perched a cap with a narrow brim. Jem knew that under the cap, Nathan had slicked his hair down with Dr. Lyman's Hair Tonic. Jem could smell it from clear up on the wagon seat. He wrinkled his nose in disgust.

Nathan reached inside his suit coat and pulled out a piece of paper and a pencil stub. "I'm a businessman now, so I figured I ought to look like one and make an impression on our customers. I brought along paper to record the dollar amounts we take in. It's important to keep records if we're going into business together."

"Oh, you're gonna make an impression, all right." Jem clasped Nathan's outstretched hand and helped him up. "They'll take one look at you and scream, 'Greenhorn! City boy!'" He shook his head and released the brake. "And just when I thought you were starting to adjust to life in Goldtown. What are you trying to do? Turn everything you've learned the past two months upside down?"

Nathan didn't answer. His face fell, and Jem immediately felt sorry for his quick tongue. But hang it all! A boy couldn't walk around a dusty, rowdy gold camp all slicked up on a weekday and not end up the worse for it. *After all,* Jem thought, *now that Pa's the sheriff, I can't have the town laughing at his nephew.*

Jem and his sister, Ellie, had not known what to expect when Aunt Rose and Nathan invaded their lives last spring. Pa had seemed thrilled to welcome his older sister into their humble ranch home, but his children had not been happy. Their pale, skinny cousin knew nothing about mining gold, ranching, or any useful chores.

However, to Jem's surprise, Nathan turned out to be a determined—if a bit slow—learner. He'd even proved himself last month, when he was forced to make his way alone through the wild and unfamiliar foothills to fetch help for an injured Strike-it-rich Sam.

But that would all be undone if Nathan paraded through town, delivering firewood in his Sunday-go-to-meeting clothes. *I reckon it's up to me to protect both our reputations,* Jem decided with a sigh. *But it's best if I do it after we leave the ranch. Otherwise, Aunt Rose might—*

"Jeremiah!" His aunt's high, demanding voice sliced into Jem's mental plans.

"Don't worry about it for now," he whispered to Nathan, then turned to his aunt. "Yes, ma'am?" He set the wagon brake and waited, although he was itching to be on his way. Aunt Rose was never quick when she had something to say, and she expected Jem's undivided attention when she did speak.

Aunt Rose stepped outside on the porch. She was a small woman, hardly up to Pa's shoulder, but she had plenty of energy to manage her brother's small ranch. Aunt Rose was pretty good at managing Jem's and Ellie's lives too. "How long are you boys going to be gone?" she asked, lifting a hand to shade her eyes from the glaring sun. "The garden needs watering. The beans are wilting on the poles."

Jem groaned and slumped in his seat. His small pouch of gold flakes and nuggets hadn't grown much lately. He could only pan Cripple Creek in snatches. That ol' garden was thirsty morning, noon, and night.

"None of that, Jeremiah Isaiah," Aunt Rose scolded. "I want you two back here in plenty of time to water. Afterward, you are free to hobnob with that filthy old miner out on your claim. But not before."

Jem was about to agree—just so he could get going— when a small figure flung open the screen door. "I got the dishes wiped, Auntie," Ellie burst out. "Can I go now? Please?" Without waiting for a reply, she scurried down the steps and hauled herself over the side and into the wagon bed. Then she climbed across the firewood and squeezed in next to Nathan on the wagon seat.

Aunt Rose frowned. "Ellianna, it would be best if . . ." Then she let out a long, resigned sigh. "Oh, go along with you." She clucked her tongue, gave a careless wave, and went back inside the house. Jem knew that behind his aunt's hard outer shell of fussing and scolding, she was as soft as warm butter—especially with Ellie.

Jem wished his sister would stay home, but now he was stuck with her. *If I don't get going soon, the dog might want to tag along too!* A quick glance showed Nugget sprawled out on the shady porch, fast asleep.

Jem released the brake and urged the horses forward. "Listen here, Ellie," he said. "You can come, but since we're not delivering frog legs, you've got no say in things. It's *firewood* today."

Ellie didn't answer. Jem peeked around Nathan and scowled at her. "Did you hear me?"

"I don't care a whit about your firewood business," she told him, brushing a short auburn braid away from her shoulder. "I'm hitchin' a ride to Maybelle's to play."

"Sure you are," Jem muttered, too low for Ellie to hear. Maybelle Sterling, just like her brother Will, never had much to do with the Coulter kids. The mine owner's family lived in a fancy house up on Belle Hill. The Coulters barely scraped by on a rundown ranch a couple miles out of town. If Ellie was going to Maybelle's to play, Jem was pretty sure Maybelle knew nothing about it.

But the Sterlings are my best firewood customers, he reminded himself. They paid top dollar for stove wood, and their cook always slipped Jem a little extra in the way of baked goods. It was worth putting up with Will if it meant keeping the Sterlings' business.

Halfway to town, Jem pulled the horses to a stop under the wide, spreading branches of an oak tree. "You really don't want to deliver firewood in those clothes," he told Nathan.

"That's the gospel truth," Ellie added.

Nathan looked ready to give in. He nodded and removed his cap. "What do you suggest?"

"The coat and tie have to go," Jem said. "It's too hot to wear them, anyway."

Nathan shed his coat and yanked off the tie. "Better?"

"Roll your sleeves up," Ellie suggested. Then she reached up and mussed his hair. "Ugh! Your hair's stiff as a fence post. Now my hands stink like greasy ol' hair tonic." She rubbed them along the sides of her dress.

"That's better," Jem said with a satisfied nod. "Much, much better. At least none of the other fellas will poke fun at you . . . or me."

"I don't feel much like a businessman now," Nathan complained. He propped his elbows on his knees and rested his chin in his hands. "More like a dirty, poor, no-account kid peddling firewood."

Jem slapped the reins, and the wagon lurched forward. He laughed. "That's what we are, Cousin." *But we won't always be!* Jem promised himself.

Even though the Coulter gold claim was pretty much played out, Jem hoped for another strike somewhere, some day. Right now, he wished he were swirling his gold pan . . .

or rocking a cradle . . . or pouring dirt, gravel, and water through a sluice box. Instead, he was hauling firewood for folks who could afford to pay somebody else to chop it up for them.

"I betcha Will has never split a piece of firewood in his entire life," Jem grumbled, losing his laughter from a minute ago. He turned the corner onto Main Street, his thoughts miles away in the gold fields. *A ten-pound gold nugget would be a mighty fine strike. I could tell Will to go chop his own—*

"Jem! Look out!"

Ellie's shriek shattered Jem's daydreaming. A small figure had darted into the street, pushing a large, rickety cart for all he was worth. Behind him, four or five older boys gave chase.

Jem jammed his feet against the floorboard and hauled back on the reins. The wagon jerked to a standstill. The horses snorted and tossed their heads against the restraints, and Jem tightened his grip. "Easy, Copper. Settle down, Silver."

Ellie looked at her brother with wide, hazel eyes. "That was close."

Jem nodded, but he couldn't keep his hands from shaking. If Pa ever found out he'd been woolgathering while driving the team, his days of using the wagon would be over. Worse, what if he'd injured or killed someone? *Thank you, God, for Ellie's quick wits!*

With his heart still hammering, Jem hopped down from the seat and stepped in front of the horses to face his mistake. He breathed a sigh of relief. *God is surely with me today.* None of the boys were injured. They stood in a clump, gaping at the restless horses a hair's breadth away.

One boy found his voice. "You tryin' to trample us, Jem?"

"Hey, Tom, I'm sorry. I . . ." His voice trailed off when he recognized the object of the boys' chase. Jem's friend Wu Shen stood a few feet away, trembling. His cart had tipped over onto its side; a pile of once snow-white laundry lay scattered at his feet.

No wonder Wu Shen had fled into the street. Jem turned on his schoolmates. "You leave Shen alone or I *will* trample you."

Tom sneered. "Or squeal to your sheriff daddy on account of one dirty China boy?"

Jem clutched Copper's bridle to keep his fist out of Tom's face. Before he could think of a good retort, the bullies whooped and took off running. Jem ignored their mocking laughter and joined the Chinese boy near his overturned cart. "I'm sorry, Shen. I wasn't paying attention. I'm glad you're not hurt."

Wu Shen gave Jem a weak smile. "You and your wagon kept boys away. I fine." Slowly, matter-of-factly, he bent over and began picking up the linens.

Jem rushed to help. He righted the cart and helped his friend refill it with the now soiled laundry. He tried to apologize again.

Wu Shen shrugged. "No problem. I do over." He lifted the handles of the pushcart and patiently set off the way he'd come, back toward his uncle's Chinese laundry.

Jem watched Shen go. He didn't understand it. Those boys were meaner than a nest of rattlesnakes, yet Wu Shen didn't yell at them or curse them or even fight back. Jem felt himself redden. *I was sure ready to go after them. Wu Shen turns the other cheek better than I do, and I'm a Christian.*

His conscience stirred. *I grumble about having no time to play around panning for gold, but Shen works hard all the time. When he's not washing laundry, he's carting supplies to his family's gold diggings.*

Suddenly, even school looked better to Jem than being in Wu Shen's shoes.

Jem climbed back on the wagon to join Ellie and Nathan,

who quietly waited for his return. He flicked a sideways glance at Nathan. Ellie would keep this mishap to herself, but Jem wasn't sure about his cousin. Maybe it was time to find out if Nathan could keep his mouth shut.

"Nathan," he began, "about what just happened. I—"

"Shhh!" Ellie ordered.

Jem rounded on his sister. "Don't tell me to—"

"Listen!" she interrupted again.

All three sat still, listening. Then Jem shrugged. "I don't hear anything." He heard nothing out of the ordinary, anyway—just harnesses jingling, a stray gunshot, horses neighing, and the occasional shouts of fights and arguing in the street.

"I know," Ellie said. "That's what I mean. It's *so quiet*."

Then Jem heard it too. The sound of silence—an eerie silence that could turn Goldtown into a ghost town.

⊰ CHAPTER 2 ⊱

An Eerie Silence

For a full minute, Jem sat still, not believing what he could no longer hear. The huge stamp mill on the hill outside town *never* rested, not even on Sunday. Ore from the Midas mine was constantly being brought to the surface and crushed under the heavy metal weights. There was no other way to begin the process of separating the tiny gold particles from the quartz rock.

The machine's banging clamor could be heard for miles—day and night—overshadowing all other sounds. When the mill first started up, Jem had hated the constant *clang, clang, clang.* He couldn't escape the noise. It followed him to school, to church, to the creek, and back to the ranch. Now, nearly a year later, he'd grown used to the background "music" of the mill and paid it no mind. It was the heartbeat of Goldtown. It meant the mine was producing gold, and lots of it.

But what if Goldtown's heart stopped beating?

Nathan broke the silence with a loud sigh. "It's about time. I am *so* tired of hearing that racket. It's enough to chase a body out of the gold fields and back to the States. Maybe we can have some peace now."

Jem wanted to agree with his cousin, but he knew better. The Midas mine provided the jobs so many people in Goldtown depended on. No mine, no miners; no miners, no need for shopkeepers, blacksmiths, teachers, barkeeps, or . . . sheriffs. Jem swallowed. "The stamp mill shutting down can't mean anything good."

As much as Jem wished the town could return to the way it was during the "boom days" of the Gold Rush, the mining of easy placer gold from the creeks and hillsides was over. Pa often reminded Jem that the future of Goldtown lay in hard-rock, underground mining. That meant the Midas mine.

Jem shaded his eyes and glanced up at Belle Hill, which rose just beyond the town. He couldn't see the mine or the stamp mill, but he knew they were there. Not far away, half-way up the hill, lay one of Jem's destinations this afternoon—the Sterling mansion. It was a fancy place, but Jem couldn't figure out why Will's family lived so close to all that noise. *If I were that rich, I would've moved the minute the mill went up.*

"Maybe something broke," Ellie said. "They'll fix it, and tomorrow it'll bang like always." She grinned. "Then we'll gripe about the noise all over again."

Jem hoped so. Either way, there was nothing *he* could do about it. He had firewood to deliver—and fast—if he wanted time for himself this afternoon. "I think we'll deliver Mr. Morrison's load first," he decided.

"Why?" Ellie wrinkled her forehead. "The Wilsons live just a few blocks over. Mr. Morrison's place is way—"

"You've got no say in how I manage my firewood business," Jem reminded her. "If you're gonna interfere, I'll leave you here, and you can walk back to the ranch."

Ellie clamped her jaw shut and glared at Jem. He waited. The tiny nod she gave him a minute later told him she'd keep her opinions to herself, at least for the rest of the deliveries.

Jem chirruped to the horses and turned the wagon

toward the road that led out of town and up Belle Hill. "It might not be a bad idea to head up there and see what's going on," he said. "Mr. Morrison will know if the stamp mill is closed down for repairs or for a more serious reason. After all, he's the mine superintendent."

"As if he'd tell *you*," Ellie muttered. She still looked mad about being bossed.

"He might," Jem said. "Maybe I'll ask him when I make my delivery." He'd unload Mr. Morrison's firewood, stack it neat as a pin, and politely ask for his money. Then, just before he turned to go, he'd ask—real casual-like—why things were so quiet. *Yes sirree, that'll work!*

It didn't take long to climb the narrow, winding road up to the Midas mine, the stamp mill, and Mr. Morrison's residence. As they climbed, a few tall, straight pines shaded their route. But most of the trees had been cut down and used to shore up the mine. The deeper they cut a tunnel of gold into the earth, the more supporting beams were needed. Blasting their way inch by inch, the miners followed the elusive vein of gold until it disappeared altogether.

Surely the gold in the Midas hasn't played out yet, Jem thought as he urged the horses around an especially steep turn.

Jem knew it took a lot of money to start up a mine. It took even more money to build a stamp mill later on to process the ore into pure gold. Mr. Sterling was rich, but he wasn't *that* rich. It was rumored he'd found a wealthy rancher down south to invest in the Midas mine with him.

Jem didn't know if the rumor was true or not. The way Will made it sound, it was *his* family's mine. His father was the owner, and that was that.

Ellie's sigh brought Jem around. "What's wrong?"

He didn't need to ask. Through the scattered trees, Jem saw Will's house in the distance. It poked out of the hill, pure white and surrounded by plenty of greenery. The trees might shield the house from the barren site of the mine and stamp mill, but nothing could shield it from the noise.

"Sure is pretty," Ellie said.

Jem frowned. "I like our place better. It's not so stiff and formal-looking." He hurried the team past the buildings clumped around the mine. The towering stamp mill rose three stories to their left, taking up most of the view. It looked deserted, but the murmur of angry voices coming from inside told Jem otherwise. He didn't slow down to listen.

The superintendent's home lay a couple hundred yards past the mine complex, nestled in a clump of oaks and young pines. Jem pulled the wagon up to the kitchen entrance and jumped down. "I'll start unloading, and you take care of business," he ordered.

When Nathan gave him a puzzled look, Jem sighed. "Knock on the door and tell Mrs. Morrison—or whoever answers the door—that we're delivering their wood. Then help me get it stacked."

Nathan nodded. A minute later, a plump, friendly woman opened the door. She took one look at the delivery boy and said, "What happened to Jem? I thought he—"

"Right here, ma'am," Jem called from the woodpile under the eaves. "He's my cousin, Nathan. I'm breaking him in."

Mrs. Morrison smiled. "Yes, I can see that." With his greased hair sticking up and his good shirt sleeves rolled up, Nathan did indeed look "broke in."

Twenty minutes later, hot and sweaty from stacking a week's worth of cooking fuel, Jem and Nathan gladly accepted lemonade from Mrs. Morrison. Ellie hopped down to grab her share of the generous gift.

However, lemonade was all Mrs. Morrison could offer them.

"I'm sorry, boys," she said when Nathan whipped out his paper and pencil to settle accounts. "Mr. Morrison forgot to set aside your money before he left this morning. He hasn't come home for the noon meal, either." She shrugged, a little nervously it seemed to Jem. "And I've no cash in my jar today."

Jem's heart sank. He'd delivered wood to the Morrisons every week for the past year, and he'd never been put off like this before. He didn't know how to respond. "I reckon I could come by tomorrow," he offered.

The woman nodded. "That might be best. Mr. Morrison's had a lot on his mind this past week." She smiled and began to close the door. "Good day."

"Mrs. Morrison," Jem said quickly. "Why is the mill shut down? Did something break?"

A worried look passed over her face. "I'm not sure, Jem. There's been some unrest at the mine, but I don't know anything about it."

"Yes, ma'am. Good-bye," Jem said, touching the brim of

his hat. He didn't believe Mrs. Morrison for a second. Her husband ran the mine. She must know plenty, but it looked like her lips were sealed tight.

Jem stepped off the porch, snagged Nathan and Ellie, and headed back to the wagon.

"That's it?" Nathan hissed in Jem's ear as they climbed aboard. "All that work and we have to come back tomorrow for our pay? That's not right."

"Oh, stop bellyaching," Jem said. He picked up the reins and set the horses in motion. "What am I supposed to do, have her arrested for not paying us this minute? Can you see Pa agreeing to *that*?"

Ellie giggled. "Pa would make you give her the whole load for free. It's best to just ride out tomorrow and collect the money."

Jem nodded his agreement. "Don't worry, Nathan. The Morrisons are good for it. Besides"—he smiled—"I have an idea how to get paid today *and* find out what's going on." Jem couldn't help it. He was burning up with curiosity to know why the stamp mill had gone silent.

"How?" Ellie and Nathan asked together.

"I'm going to stop by the mining office and ask Mr. Morrison for my pay. He'll be so sorry he forgot to leave it that he'll apologize all over the place. Then I'll ask him about the stamp mill." Jem laughed. "They call that 'killing two birds with one stone.'" He urged the team back the way they'd come.

"I think we should go up the road and make the Sterlings' delivery first," Ellie said. "You can stop by the office on the way back."

Jem gave Ellie his what-did-I-tell-you-about-interfering look and kept driving.

By the time they pulled up to the mining office, the angry sounds Jem had heard from the stamp mill earlier had increased in volume. *Somebody's spittin' mad about something,*

Jem thought, slowing the team to a halt. He set the brake, wrapped the reins around the handle, and hopped down. "Stay put. I'll be right back."

The mining office looked empty. Jem hoped Mr. Morrison was inside, working on the day's accounts or setting up mining schedules, or whatever it was a mining superintendent did all day. Jem knew what Mr. Sterling, the mine *owner* did—all the clean, behind-the-scenes work, which earned him a lot of money.

The superintendent did all the hard work, like keeping the miners working and contented. It couldn't be an easy job. Who wanted to crawl around in dank, dimly lit passages? Who wanted to run like mad and hope you didn't get blown up when setting off the blasting powder to enlarge the mine? Jem shivered. *Not me!* He was glad Pa had traded his gold pan for a ranch and a sheriff's badge, although two months ago Jem would not have admitted it.

Jem sprinted to the office and turned the knob. "It's locked!" he said in surprise. Why would the office be locked and empty? It was the middle of a workday. He peeked through a window next to the door and saw nothing that might explain the closure.

"Mr. Morrison!" he called, rapping on the window. "Are you in there? I've come for my firewood money."

No one answered.

Before Jem could decide what to do next, a sudden roar erupted from the nearby stamp mill. A stream of nearly a hundred dirty, shouting miners burst from the building. "We want our pay! We want our pay!" they chanted. The men surged across the compound carrying clubs, hammers, and pickaxes. They looked ready to break into the mining office and find their wages for themselves.

Oh, please, God, no! Jem prayed in horror. *Not a riot! Not here!*

Jem had seen his share of saloon fights, where rowdy drunks went after each other. He'd seen for himself what lawless claim jumpers like Frenchy DuBois would do to keep their stolen gold diggings. But it was nothing compared to what he saw now. The size of this crowd turned Jem's blood to ice and set his feet flying.

It was time to leave—and fast.

CHAPTER 3

Riot!

Jem leaped from the porch and landed at the foot of the steps. *Hurry! Back to the wagon!* he ordered his wobbly legs. He saw Ellie and Nathan on the wagon seat. They sat frozen, staring at the mob swarming toward the office. In moments, the men would overwhelm the small building and tear into it.

Ellie's face was ashen. Jem knew why. He had to pass in front of the crowd to reach the safety of the wagon.

Crash! The tinkle of broken glass warned Jem that the men meant business. They would not pause to let him pass; they probably didn't even see him in their eagerness to storm the office. Jem picked up his pace . . . and lost his footing. He stumbled to the ground, caught himself, and stood up, breathing hard. His heart pounded.

He was cut off.

Jem whirled and dodged to his right. A rock whizzed past his ear. He ducked and ran. Snatches of conversation burned his ears: "Let's string 'em up!" "Get the strong box!" "They can't get away with this!" "We'll show 'em." "Hang 'em *all!*"

Suddenly, the ear-piercing shriek of the mine's alarm drowned out the men's shouts. Jem knew the whistle blew only for the most dire of emergencies, like a mine cave-in or an accident. Somebody was pulling it now, screaming for help from the town below.

The whistle did not slow the men down. They rushed up the porch steps and began breaking down the door with their pickaxes and hammers. More glass shattered.

Jem skirted the edge of the crowd and tried to reach the wagon. The men had spread out in a loose semicircle, surrounding the mine office. Rocks—and fists—continued to fly. *Where's Mr. Morrison? Or Mr. Sterling?* Jem wondered. *Or any of the supervisors?* He saw an opening and slipped past a few stragglers.

Then everything happened at once. A man staggered backward, slamming into him. Jem tried to skip out of the way, but he was not quick enough. A rock—or a fist—slammed into his head. Jem crumpled to the ground. He heard Ellie scream.

His world went dark.

Where am I? Jem took a few deep breaths, just to make sure he was still in one piece. *What's going on?* Somebody was dragging him across a bumpy, rock-filled road. *A road? No, more like a—*

Jem groaned when whoever was yanking on him let him drop. His head exploded with pain. He felt more pushing, more shoving. He made a feeble attempt to kick his assailants, to make them leave him alone. "Let me go!" he gasped. "I want Pa."

"He'll be here in no time," Ellie told him. "They blew the whistle. That'll bring Pa—and half the town."

Jem opened his eyes and squinted at his sister. She was rubbing her eyes, like she'd been crying. He looked around and found himself lying on his back under the wagon. Ellie and Nathan sat hunched on either side of him. "What happened?" Jem whispered.

Nathan answered. "A rock hit you, and down you went. There was nothing we could do until the crowd thinned out. Half the miners broke into the office. The other half took off up the road."

"I think they're heading to the Sterlings," Ellie said.

Jem couldn't believe this was happening. He knew most of these men. Many had been prospectors during Goldtown's boom days, before they went to work in the mine. As a little boy, Jem had crouched next to them in the creek, watching them pan for gold. He had listened, wide-eyed, to their gold tales. Dry Dirt McGee, Pepper Pete, Plug Nickel Jim, the others—they were his friends. Jem went to school with their children. What would turn these men into a mindless mob?

Jem's head hurt too much to figure it out. He lay still and wished he were home in bed instead of covered with fine dust, hiding under a wagon. The horses snorted and stamped their hooves. "I set the brake, right?" he murmured.

Being run over would be a fitting end to this miserable day. He had only made one firewood delivery, and he hadn't even been paid. Two customers were waiting for their orders. If he didn't deliver, he'd lose their business. His gold pan sat on the porch, ready for an hour or two of wading in the creek and panning for gold with Strike. For once, he didn't feel like it.

Oh, yeah. And I almost ran over my friend, Shen. Jem smiled weakly. *But I bet I get out of hauling water for Aunt Rose this afternoon.*

Small comfort.

Crashing and scuffling came from the mine office. Jem rolled onto his stomach and peeked out from under the wagon. Something warm dribbled down the side of his cheek. He smeared his hand across his face and brought it away red and sticky. He winced. *No wonder my head hurts!*

"I hope Mr. Morrison's all right," Ellie whispered. She

was shaking. "Why are they yelling and fighting and tearing things up, Jem?"

"I . . . don't know," Jem said. It hurt too much to talk. He closed his eyes and rested his head on his arms. "Leave me alone."

"I know why," Nathan said. "I saw something like this in Boston. A group of factory workers rioted and tore things up. They wanted their jobs back after machines started taking over in the factories. It didn't do 'em any good. The machines were there to stay. But it was scary. I was just a little kid, and I still remember it." He shuddered. "It sounds like these miners want to get paid."

Ellie frowned. "Why wouldn't they be?"

Jem stirred. "Maybe the mine's played out. No gold . . . no money." He fell quiet. The crashing and yelling kept up. He wished they would all go away. The men were fools if they thought Mr. Morrison kept thousands of dollars in the office just for the taking. *I'm so tired . . .*

"It's Pa!" Ellie squealed.

Dust flew in Jem's face as his sister scrambled out from under the wagon. He forced his eyes open. A dozen horsemen were pounding up the hill, with Pa in the lead on King. The sheriff held up his hand, and the men pulled their mounts to a stop in front of the mine office. When he dismounted and yanked his rifle from its scabbard, Jem knew Pa had lost no time figuring out the situation.

Three shots in the air brought the scuffling from inside the office to a standstill. The whistle alarm had stopped its piercing call a few minutes before.

"Pa!" Ellie shouted into the silence.

Pa whirled. His eyes widened at the sight of the Coulter wagon and Ellie running toward him. "Get back!" he ordered. Then he returned his attention to what was left of the small building.

Ellie skidded to a stop, turned tail, and dived back under the wagon.

Jem couldn't hear what his father was saying. Pa didn't yell at the men when they streamed from the office. The miners stood around in dejected-looking clumps, their anger and frustration clearly spent.

Pa clapped a miner on the shoulder and shook his head. He motioned another over and said something. The man nodded, head bowed. When questioned, he pointed beyond the trees, toward the Sterling place.

Pa gathered the miners into a group and left three armed deputies to guard them. Then he raised his voice. "Josh, you and Frank find Morrison and make sure he's all right. The rest of you, go after the others. Let them know there will be no more looting or destruction of mine property. Tell them I said you can shoot 'em to show I mean business. Get going, before they scare Morrison's wife half to death. I'll go see Sterling and find out what's going on."

The men took off.

Pa turned and stalked to the wagon. He leaned his rifle against the wheel and crouched down. "What in blazes are you kids doing here?" he demanded. "Get out from under there. I oughta tan your hides."

Ellie and Nathan scrambled to obey. Jem wanted to obey Pa too, but his arms and legs wouldn't do what he told them. He felt as weak as a newborn calf—all from one poorly aimed rock. *Don't lie here like a limp string. Crawl!*

But he couldn't.

Pa was still scolding. "You could've been—"

"Jem's hurt, Pa," Ellie interrupted. "A rock bashed him in the head."

Instantly, Pa was on his hands and knees, gently easing Jem out from under the wagon. Jem blinked in the bright sunlight. "I'm s-sorry, Pa. I was trying to collect my fire—"

25

"Don't talk, Son," Pa said, his voice calm and soothing. "It's all right." He set Jem up and leaned him against the wagon wheel. Then he whistled. "That's some souvenir you've got, boy." He untied the bandana from around his neck and dabbed at the blood.

Jem yelped and jerked his head away. Unwanted tears stung his eyes. "Pa! That *hurts!*"

"I'm sorry, Jeremiah," Pa said softly. "I'm no doctor." He stuffed the neckerchief into his back pocket. "I reckon you'll just have to bleed 'til I can get you some proper care. Can you stand?"

Jem didn't know if he could stand or not, but he had to try. He couldn't be *that* injured. It wasn't like he'd been shot or anything. Why, just a few weeks ago, part of a flume had fallen on him! He'd shaken it off and gone on to rescue his sister. Surely, one rock—no matter how hard it had hit him—could not keep him down for long.

Jem let Pa help him to his feet, but a wave of dizziness nearly drowned him. He swayed, and Pa caught him up in his arms. "I've got you. Just relax."

"Why do I feel so woozy?"

"When you see yourself in the mirror, you'll know why," Nathan put in. "The whole side of your face is turning into one, big, bloody—"

"That will do," Pa warned. He hugged Jem tight, then lifted him up to the wagon seat. Before Jem had a chance to topple over, his father was right beside him, steadying him. "Hand up my rifle and climb in," he called to Ellie and Nathan. "We'll go to the Sterlings to tend Jem's injury. Then I'll find out what's going on at the mine."

Leaving his horse in the deputies' hands, Pa stashed his rifle in the wagon bed and picked up the reins. With one hand he got the wagon moving. He kept his other arm tightly around Jem. "Hang on. It's not far."

Jem leaned against his father, gritted his teeth, and prayed the jolting ride would end soon. Each jerk of the wagon over the rough road shot pain through his head. Surprised squeals from the wagon bed told him that Ellie and Nathan were not enjoying the trip either. Pa was definitely in a hurry.

The road passed the Morrison place. Pa barely lifted the reins in greeting as he drove by. Goldtown's temporary deputies were there, rounding up a group of miners. Jem squinted. Was that Mrs. Morrison standing on the porch, pointing a *shotgun* at the men? Then a deep chuckle from Pa made Jem want to smile too. Mrs. Morrison could probably take care of herself.

A few minutes later, Pa pulled the wagon to a stop in front of a stately, glistening white mansion. The driveway continued around back, where Jem usually made his firewood deliveries. Today, however, Pa wasn't messing with minor details like where the hired help were expected to knock. He set the brake and jumped down from the wagon. Then he grabbed Jem and carried him up the front steps.

"Pa," Ellie said in a small voice. "This is the front door. We're s'posed to go 'round to—"

The door opened to Pa's knock.

The housekeeper, a tall, thin woman with gray hair and dark eyes, blinked her surprise. "Sheriff Coulter. Good afternoon. What can I do for you?"

"My son is hurt. I need a place to tend him," Pa said. "I've come to see Ernest as well. Mine business."

"By all means," she replied instantly. "Come in."

Jem felt like a fool. What if Will saw him, helpless and being carried like he was five years old?

The next instant, Maybelle Sterling's huffy voice broke in on the adults. "Ellianna, what are you doing here? And why is your brother dripping blood all over our front entry?"

⊰ CHAPTER 4 ⊱

The Sterlings

Ellie planted her fists on her hips and stepped into the house. "Jem's here to deliver your firewood," she told Maybelle. "But he got hurt. So Nathan and I have to unload it. You want to help?"

Jem admired his little sister's spunk. He could count on the fingers of one hand how many times he and Ellie had been invited into the Sterling home. Yet, instead of being enchanted by the high ceilings, inlaid wood floors, and fancy fixtures, Ellie ignored it all and got right down to business.

Maybelle sucked in her breath. "Me? Carry firewood? Goodness, no!"

"Miss Maybelle, fetch some rags for Sheriff Coulter," the housekeeper broke in. She turned to Pa. "You can settle the boy in the parlor, right through there." She pointed to a doorway. "I'll let Mr. Sterling know you're here."

She fluttered down the hall like a hen after her chicks.

"The rags are to keep all that blood off Mother's good couch," Maybelle said. Her gaze flicked to the splattered drops on the hardwood floor. "But you really shouldn't use the par—"

"The quicker you get those rags," Pa reminded her, "the

quicker Jem will stop bleeding all over your fine floor." He smiled.

"Yes, sir." Maybelle turned and hurried after the housekeeper.

Jem knew Pa's smile was forced. Sheriff Coulter did not like dealing with the snobbish rich folks up on the Hill. He would much rather break up fights in the saloons and gambling halls, arrest claim jumpers, or even track down thieves and murderers.

Jem agreed. Ever since he'd discovered his father was a crack shot, he no longer lay awake nights worrying if lawbreakers would try to rid Goldtown of its new, interfering sheriff. Pa could take care of himself. *Outlaws, beware!*

Pa carried Jem into the parlor. "Give me patience," he muttered under his breath, looking heavenward. Then he sighed, long and deep.

"Sorry, Pa," Jem said. His father sighed like that when he was faced with a particularly unpleasant task ahead. Jem had a feeling that what he'd seen today had no quick, easy fix.

"Not your fault," Pa said. "You were in the wrong spot at the wrong time. I'm just glad you're all right. It could have been a lot worse."

"I meant that I know how you feel about coming up here and—"

Running footsteps and Pa's warning look kept the rest of Jem's words inside his mouth. As much as he and Will disliked each other, Jem was a guest in his home. Pa did not care for the Sterlings either, but he treated all citizens of Goldtown with courtesy and respect. Today would be a good day for Jem to follow his father's example.

Maybelle scurried into the parlor, her arms full of rags. She spread them over the settee cushions just as her father appeared in the doorway.

"Matt!" Mr. Sterling exclaimed. "What happened?"

Will and Mrs. Sterling entered the parlor behind him and watched the sheriff settle Jem on the couch. Celia, the youngest Sterling, clutched her mother's skirt and peeped at the visitors.

Pa straightened. "Jem was caught in a riot up at the mine. Surely you heard the alarm?"

Mr. Sterling's face paled. He nodded. "I was just on my way out the door to find Morrison. A riot, you say? How in *blazes* did the superintendent let something like that happen?" His voice sounded full of righteous anger. "I pay him to keep order." He paused and motioned the housekeeper into the room.

She was carrying a pan of water and more rags. "Do you want me to send for Dr. Martin?" she asked.

Pa shot Jem an anxious, undecided look.

Mr. Sterling brushed Pa's worries aside. "Mrs. Anders has nursed many a miner," he assured him. "She'll fix your son up."

Jem lay back and closed his eyes. It felt good to lie on soft coverings, surrounded by the low babble of familiar voices. *Now, if everybody will go away and leave me alone for a few minutes!*

No such luck. Gentle hands—not like Pa's clumsy attempts—began to wipe his face. Warm water washed away the blood and dirt. Jem relaxed and let Mrs. Anders clean him up.

"I don't think we need the doctor," she decided. "He'll hurt for a few days, but with a bit of care, he should heal up fine. Now, just one more thing to do."

The warning in Mrs. Anders's voice set Jem's nerves tingling. He smelled the sharp bite of iodine just before a glob of soaked cotton touched his head. *Augh! It stings worse than a rope burn!*

Jem gritted his teeth and squeezed his eyes shut. Not a whimper escaped his lips. After all, Will was standing just across the room. Jem was not about to let the Sterling boy see him blubber like a girl. He lay still, although he wanted to thrash and scream and kick at the hand dabbing the iodine on his wound.

Then it was over. A soft bandage replaced the cold medicine, and Mrs. Anders tied a strip of cloth around Jem's head to hold the bandage in place. He opened his eyes. "Thank you, ma'am."

The housekeeper nodded. "You need to lie still awhile. Then your father can take you home." She heaped the soiled rags in the pan of dirty water and stood up. "You'd best let somebody else finish your firewood route today." She flashed Jem a smile and hurried from the room.

As soon as she left, everybody crowded around Jem. Pa gave him a wink and a nod that meant, *You did good*. Maybelle and little Celia scuttled over and stared, but Will hung back.

Ellie leaned over and whispered in Jem's ear. "Think of it, Jem! You're restin' in a real parlor."

Jem reddened and hoped nobody else heard Ellie's silly remark. He felt like a helpless, pampered fool and couldn't wait to get back to his own bed up in his own attic. Nathan didn't say anything, but it didn't take much figuring to know what his cousin was thinking. The rest of the firewood route was on Nathan's shoulders now. He didn't look happy.

Pa reached down and squeezed Jem's shoulder. Then he turned to Mr. Sterling. "We'd better talk, Ernest. It looks like you have a problem on your hands. If I'm to keep order in town, I need to know what's going on."

Mr. Sterling nodded. "I agree. First of all—"

Pa's eyebrows shot up. "Shouldn't we go someplace else to talk?"

"What I have to tell you won't take long," Mr. Sterling said with a frown. "And I'll decide where I say it. The parlor is fine. Your son can rest, and"—he nodded at Will—"Will can keep him company while you and I discuss matters. Maybelle?"

"Yes, Father?"

"Take these youngsters up to the playroom and show them your toys. Sheriff Coulter and I do not wish to be disturbed."

"Do I *have* to?" She scrunched up her face.

"*Now!*" her father shouted.

The children scattered. All except Will. He edged closer to the couch but kept his gaze on the retreating figures of his sisters, Ellie, and Nathan. He looked like he wished he could go with them.

Mrs. Sterling followed the group and closed the door behind her with a soft *click*.

An awkward silence fell over the room, but it was soon filled with the grown-ups' droning voices. They moved off to a couple of easy chairs near a large bay window, leaving the boys alone.

Jem closed his eyes. He wanted to lie still and drift off, listening to Pa's voice. But his thoughts were a jumble. *I can't finish my route? Nonsense!* No rich folks' housekeeper was going to tell him he was too hurt to finish a job. He sure couldn't leave the task to Nathan and Ellie.

The cushions jiggled and Jem opened his eyes. Will sat hunched over on the edge of the couch, pouting. His unruly black curls hung over his forehead. He squinted at Jem, daring him to say something.

Jem dared. "You don't have to stick around and nursemaid me. I'm fine."

"I'd like nothing better than to get out of here," Will said. "But for some dumb reason, Father wants me to keep an eye on you. Maybe he thinks you're going to bleed right through the rags." He scowled and stood up. "I'll get the checkerboard."

Jem no more felt like playing checkers right now than he felt like panning for gold. "Don't trouble yourself on my account."

"I'm getting it for me," Will shot back. "Playing checkers with you is better than sitting here staring at you." He shuffled over to a large, ornate cabinet and rummaged around inside. When he returned, he was carrying the board and a box of checkers.

Jem sat up and made room for Will. His head throbbed a protest, but he pushed the pain aside.

Will set up the game. "Go on. Your move first."

Jem hesitated. He had never in his wildest dreams seen himself sharing a checkerboard with Will Sterling. Most of his thoughts about Will—when he took the trouble to think about him at all—centered around how to avoid the mine owner's weasel-faced son. Will had a talent for making Jem feel like he lived on the bottom rung of life's ladder. And being the sheriff's son? A terrible misfortune, Will insisted. It must be hard to be "good" all the time.

Too often, their encounters ended in sharp words and hard feelings, and occasionally in bruised knuckles.

"You gonna stare at the board all day?" Will asked. "Or are you gonna move?"

Jem slid a red checker to the next square, but his heart was not in the game. He couldn't figure out why Will would want to play checkers with him today . . . or any day. Maybe it *was* better than staring at each other while their fathers talked, but not by much.

Every now and then, Will's gaze flicked to the two men sitting at the far side of the room. His mind didn't appear to be on the game either. He seemed anxious and edgy.

Jem's interest rose a notch. Did Will know what was going on with his father's mine, or why the stamp mill had shut down? *Probably.* Will loved to stick his nose into everybody's business—like the time he fetched the new sheriff when Jem and Ellie played hooky from school.

But will he tell me anything?

A sudden idea made Jem jump one of Will's black pieces. Then he let Will jump two of his red ones. In a matter of minutes, Jem's opponent had cleared the board of red checkers and was grinning like a possum.

He rubbed his hands together. "Another game?"

"I reckon." Jem arranged the checkers for the next round and moved his piece. "Say, Will, do you know why the stamp mill shut down? Is it for repairs?"

Will's possum grin vanished. He glanced at his father then leaned over the checkerboard. His voice dropped to a frightened whisper. "Yeah, I know why. The vein has played out. There's no more gold in the mine."

CHAPTER 5

Mine Trouble

The gold's *gone?*" Like Will, Jem kept his voice barely above a whisper. No sense letting the grown-ups get after them for talking about things boys shouldn't know. "How can that be? I thought there was enough gold in the Midas mine to last for years and years. It can't just up and vanish in a day, can it?"

Will swallowed, shot another glance at his father, and slid a checker across the board. "I don't know. But I heard Father and Mr. Morrison talking about it last week."

This was no surprise to Jem. Will was a snoop and a sneak. "I bet you didn't hear it 'round the supper table."

Will's cheeks turned red. "I was at the mining office one afternoon."

Jem snorted. "The office that's a shambles now?" When Will gave him a puzzled look, Jem pointed to the side of his face. "How do you think I got this? I stopped by to collect my firewood money from Mr. Morrison. He wasn't there. The miners smashed the windows and broke down the door. Looks like they were trying to collect *their* pay too."

Will nodded miserably. "Father and Mr. Morrison were arguing real loud about money. I couldn't help but hear. I was standing right on the front steps. I guess the last shipment of gold was so small that Father could only pay half wages. Mr. Morrison promised the men their full pay this week. He said Father would just have to come up with the money." Will winced. "You should have heard Father yell."

Jem caught his breath. The Sterlings were rich, but did they have the ready cash to pay all those miners? Even if Mr. Sterling did have the money, did he want to lose it in a worthless mining venture? Jem didn't need to ask Will such private questions. He already knew what Mr. Sterling had decided to do. Jem's throbbing head was evidence that Will's father had not paid the miners.

"Does it mean the Midas will close down for good?" Jem ignored the checkers game and searched Will's face for an answer. Surely the little eavesdropper had heard the rest of the story.

"I don't know," Will said. "But if the gold has really fizzled out, then . . ." His voice died.

Jem's stomach clenched. This news hurt worse than the iodine Mrs. Anders had dabbed on his cut. The mine couldn't shut down. Goldtown was his home. It *couldn't* become like the other ghost towns that littered the Mother Lode country. He knew their names—Mud Spring, once a gold camp of thousands, Cold Water, Savage Camp, dozens more—all abandoned by prospectors seeking fresh diggings.

"Where would we go?" Jem asked.

"It's all well and good for *you*," Will said. "Your family has that run-down ranch. You can stay here. At least you won't starve. But what about *my* folks? If we lose our mine—" He clamped his mouth shut. "I've said too much already."

You haven't said half enough! Jem wanted to shout. Questions buzzed around inside his head like a swarm of angry hornets. "What else did your father and Mr. Morrison say?" Jem didn't care if he'd just joined ranks with a sneaky spy. He had to know his town's fate.

Will swept the checkers into the box. "I don't want to play anymore," he growled and rose.

Jem grabbed his sleeve. "*Will!*"

Will shook off Jem's grasp and sat down. "I don't know anything more. There were snatches of talk about a possible new gold vein, but Mr. Morrison said it was only wishful thinking. Then I heard stomping, and I ran around the side of the office." He bowed his head and stared at his shoes. "I didn't want a thrashing."

"Maybe there *is* another vein," Jem said. "You only listened to one meeting. There must be other meetings between your father and Mr. Morrison, *something* they can do." Jem took a deep breath. "I don't want the mine to shut down either, Will. More folks than your family will suffer. Half the town depends on that mine. If everybody leaves, it'll be mighty lonely out on an ol' ranch by ourselves."

Will looked up. "Father told us at supper last night that he telegraphed the other mine owner—some rancher who lives down south. He invited him here to talk about the mine. Father said we kids better be on our best behavior." Will made a face. "I hate it when Father entertains guests."

For the second time that afternoon, Jem's eyebrows rose. Playing checkers with Will had surprised him, but hearing the boy's private thoughts astonished Jem even more. Had Will meant for Jem to hear his last remark? Probably not.

A rustling from the other side of the room told Jem that Pa and Mr. Sterling had finished their discussion.

Will looked frantic. "Father doesn't know I listened in. If you blab one word of this, I'll knock you into the next county."

"I'd like to see you try!" Then a speck of good sense made Jem lower his voice. "Nobody can keep this a secret for long. But don't worry. I'll keep your eavesdropping to myself." He disliked Will, but he would keep his word.

Pa stalked over to the boys, slapping his hat against his leg. His dark eyes flashed; a muscle twitched in his jaw.

What's eating Pa? Jem wondered with a chill.

"You feel up to walking out of here, Son?" Pa asked calmly. But Jem could see that his father was holding a tight rein on his temper.

"Yes, sir." Jem flung his legs over the side of the couch and stood up. A wave of dizziness made him stagger, but Pa caught his arm and steadied him. The dizziness passed. "Thanks for the game," he told Will.

"Don't mention it," Will mumbled, head down. He didn't look at Jem.

Pa wrapped a strong arm around Jem's shoulders and guided him across the room. When he reached the door, he yanked it open then turned back for a final word. "I'm going to ask you one more time to pay those miners *something*, Ernest. Anything. You took a chance, and you lost."

Mr. Sterling's face darkened. "I'll thank you to let me run things as I see fit, Sheriff. The mine and mill are shut down until that new vein is surveyed and we can start blasting. The men took the chance as well."

Pa tightened his grip on Jem. "My son is evidence that the men don't see it that way. They gave you an honest week's work, and they deserve to be paid. You can afford to wait for a survey and the decision to either close down for good or go deeper. The miners can't. Men with hungry families make my job even harder."

He scanned the rich furnishings of the Sterlings' parlor. "Dig a little deeper into your pockets, Ernest. One more week of half wages would be a sign of good faith. If not"—Pa sighed—"I suggest you find a deep hole to hide in. I can't protect you from the entire town."

Mr. Sterling puffed up like a turkey gobbler. "Sheriff Coulter, you are paid to protect every citizen in Goldtown. I expect protection for my property, as well. Hire the deputies you need. Do I make myself clear?"

Pa gave Mr. Sterling a curt nod. "I will do my best, sir. But I can't promise anything with the mood the miners are in." Without another word, Jem and his father left the parlor, hurried down the hallway, and saw themselves out of the Sterlings' home.

When they stood on the front porch, Jem sagged. "Mr. Sterling's awful mad."

"No, Jem," Pa told him, clapping his hat on his head. "He's just awful scared, and I can't say I blame him. He has a pile of decisions to make in the coming weeks. And none of them will be easy." He looked around. "What happened to the wagon?"

"It's probably 'round back," Jem said. "I hope Nathan unloaded the wood."

They made their way to the kitchen entrance and found Nathan and Ellie stacking the last of the order in the woodshed. Ellie slammed the door, latched it, and skipped over to Jem.

"All done." It looked like a dozen new freckles had popped out on Ellie's cheeks this afternoon. Drops of sweat glistened on her forehead. "It wasn't so bad," she bragged, grinning.

"Stacking wood is the *easy* part of the firewood business," Jem reminded her. "It's the chopping and splitting that wears you down."

Ellie lost her grin. She wrinkled her forehead, bit her lip, and gave her brother a resentful look. "I guess you're right about that."

Nathan brushed the dirt and scraps from his hands and wandered over to stand by his cousins. He looked in worse shape than Ellie. His greased hair stuck straight up, dust covered his face, and his white shirt was smeared with pitch and fine bark dust.

Pa pushed back his hat and whistled. "Rosie won't like seeing your Sunday shirt in that condition. Pine pitch is sticky and lasting. I'm not sure even boiling will get it out."

Nathan didn't seem to care. "Can we go home now? I'm hot and tired."

"Soon as I collect our pay," Ellie said. She darted to the back door. A minute later she returned with a fistful of coins and a small brown bag. "The money's for you, Jem"—she dropped the silver in her brother's hands—"and the dough-nuts are for all of us. The Sterlings' cook is a wonder."

The doughnuts smelled fresh and hot. Warm grease soaked through the paper sack. Jem's mouth watered as he reached for his share of the treat.

"You get two," Ellie told him, "on account of you being hurt an' all. Isn't Cook the nicest cook in the whole world?" She bit into her doughnut and sighed. "I'd deliver firewood in trade for doughnuts any day," she mumbled, her mouth full of the hot, tender pastry.

Jem chewed silently and studied the coins in his hand. *Fair's fair*, he decided. He divided the money equally into thirds and passed Nathan and Ellie their shares. "It looks like you'll have to deliver the load to the Wilsons too," he said. It hurt only a little to slip the small amount of leftover money into his pocket. "But just this once. By next week, I'll be fine."

Ellie gaped at the coins in her hand. "Thanks, Jem! This is more than you give me for catching frogs." She looked up at her brother. "Stacking wood was heaps more fun than sit-ting around upstairs, playing with Maybelle's silly dolls. All she wanted to do was talk about the time she went to San Francisco to see the opera. She sang me one of the songs, and I'll tell you this: Maybelle is no nightingale. More like a screeching crow."

Jem burst into laughter. So did Pa. Even Nathan cracked a smile.

"Enough," Pa finally said. "We're finished here, so let's load up and get going. I need to collect my horse, then I'll drive you to Wilsons'." Pa shook his head when Jem opened his mouth. "No, you are not driving this wagon anywhere. Not with your injury. Besides, the Wilsons live in town, and I'd just as soon you didn't deliver wood there alone today." His voice turned somber. "In fact, I want you kids to stay away from town for a while."

Pa didn't have to tell them why. Jem knew. Goldtown was a rowdy, rough-and-tumble gold camp, but most days it was safe to walk the streets. But now? With nearly a hundred restless miners out of work, the saloons would overflow. Uncertainty about the future would lead to more arguments and fistfights—maybe even robberies and gunplay.

Goldtown's sheriff would have his hands full.

Please, God, Jem prayed as Pa turned the wagon around and headed back down the hill, *let the mine reopen soon. I'll never complain about that noisy stamp mill again. Don't let Goldtown turn into a ghost town!*

CHAPTER 6

Cripple Creek

Young'un, if ya don't stop fussin' over me, I'm gonna toss ya down the nearest mining hole and leave ya there." The scruffy prospector glared at Jem from under shaggy eyebrows and reached for the contraption sitting next to him. He curled his fingers around a long handle and set the wood box on rockers into motion. Back and forth, back and forth, the cradle sifted gravel, water, dirt, and—hopefully—a gold nugget or two.

Jem dropped the bucket he was carrying. Water sloshed over the lip. "Hang it all, Strike! Panning for gold is hard enough when a fella has two good arms. How do you expect to do it with only one?"

Strike rose from his hunched-over position next to the rocker. He let go of the handle, slung a droopy suspender back in place, and lifted the pail. "Like this." Steadying the bucket on one knee, he tried pouring the contents through a screen on top of the rocker. The bucket tipped and wobbled. Most of the water missed the target and splashed on the rocks and back into Cripple Creek.

Jem shook his head. Strike-it-rich Sam was as hard-headed as his donkey, Canary. But his stubbornness was probably the only reason the miner was still alive. A little over a month ago, Strike had been left to die out in the middle of nowhere. No wonder a "little thing" like a broken arm couldn't keep him down.

"If you let me help, I wouldn't spill a drop," Jem said. "I'll pour, and you can rock."

"Nothin' doin'. You got your hands full with that cousin of yours," Strike muttered, letting the bucket clatter to the ground. He went back to working the rocker's handle with one hand. His other arm lay wrapped and splinted in a makeshift sling. He used his chin as a pointer. "Lookee there. I don't think the tenderfoot's got the hang of it yet. Leastways, he doesn't look serious."

Jem glanced at the creek in time to see Nathan take another tumble into the water. He heard Ellie's high-pitched giggle and watched the two of them turn their gold pans into weapons of war. An all-out water fight followed. Whatever gold might have been in their pans was now halfway down the creek.

There probably wasn't more than a sprinkling of gold dust anyway, Jem thought. He thrust his hand into his pocket and felt the soft, worn leather of his half-empty gold pouch. During the past week, he'd spent every afternoon at Cripple Creek, with Aunt Rose's blessing. She had clucked and fussed over Jem's injury, then let him off from any heavy chores around the ranch for a few days.

"Sitting next to the creek and swishing a gold pan is

no work," she'd told him. Which showed Jem that his aunt knew nothing about the business. Panning for gold was plenty of work. "It even sounds restful," she'd said. "Hurry along and heal quick. I need you, now that Matt is gone so much."

Jem knew the ranch was suffering, but he'd obeyed before Aunt Rose changed her mind. *My dream come true!* Or so he thought. But his heart was not in it. The silence of the abandoned stamp mill kept Jem's mind on the fate of the Midas mine—not on how much gold he could coax out of Cripple Creek. He'd found only a dozen gold flakes and four pea-sized nuggets this week.

"Pa doesn't tell me a thing," Jem complained. "He eats breakfast, grabs his hat, and rides off to town every morning." He picked up a rock and pitched it in the creek. "Nothing gets done at home. The spring calves haven't even been branded yet." He turned to see if Strike was listening. "Pa promised to teach me this year. What if they—"

"If you want to make yourself useful," Strike hollered over the rattling of the rocker, "you can fetch me a cup o' coffee."

Jem rolled his eyes. Strike hadn't heard a word he'd said. *But at least he wants a little help.* Jem was eager to give his friend a hand, even if it only meant getting coffee. He scrambled up the creek bank and over to the ring of blackened stones surrounding the prospector's campfire. It had burned low, so Jem stirred the coals and added a piece of wood. He found Strike's battered tin cup, reached for the ladle in the coffee pail . . . and stopped.

Something soggy and dark gray hung over the edge of the simmering bucket of brew. He peered closer. A sock? Careful to keep from getting burned, Jem pinched the edge of the sock and slowly lifted it up. Thick, dark liquid dripped back into the bucket. Jem brought the sock to his nose and sniffed. *Ugh!* It was stuffed with coffee grounds.

As if Strike's bitter brew wasn't disgusting enough! Jem was pretty sure the new coffee recipe did not include a *clean* sock. Strike had no clean clothes. *I bet if I look inside his boots, I'll find only one sock.*

Jem shuddered and dropped the sock back in the pail. "What kind of tomfool idea is *this*?" he wondered aloud.

"I can tell you."

Jem whirled at the laughing voice. A boy he'd never seen before stood several yards away. He was taller than Jem, and stockier, with black hair and bright blue eyes. A wide-brimmed hat perched on his head, and his fists were planted on his hips.

"Who're *you*?" Jem challenged.

The boy dropped his arms and hurried over. "Chad Carter. And you?"

"Jem Coulter."

Chad's eyes opened wide. "Your father's the sheriff."

Jem nodded.

"I met him the other day. Seems like a decent sort."

Jem bristled. Pa was a whole lot more than just a "decent sort." Then he let it go. Clearly, this strange boy was only trying to make friends. *Don't be so touchy,* Jem told himself.

"*Where's my coffee?*" Strike's raspy voice carried clear from the creek below.

"Coming!" Jem yelled back. He quickly ladled the thick, black drink into Strike's cup.

Chad pointed to the steaming pot. "The sock keeps the coffee grounds from getting in the brew. That's the way our hands make it on the trail." He grinned. "Cowboy coffee."

"Strike's not a cowboy," Jem said. He dropped the ladle back in the pot and started toward the creek.

Chad easily kept up. "Let me have a swallow." He reached for the cup.

Jem shook his head, but he was smiling. "I don't think my

pa would want me to poison a guest first thing. This is not real coffee. It's . . . well . . . just believe me. It's not drinkable."

The new boy laughed. "It can't be worse than the stuff Cooky brews on the trail."

Jem eyed the boy, then shrugged and gave in. "Suit yourself."

With a nod of thanks, Chad took a generous swallow . . . and gagged. His eyes bulged. He choked, coughed, and spewed the rest of the drink on the ground. "I was wrong," he croaked, handing the cup back, "*this* is worse." He wiped his mouth and shuddered.

Jem howled with laughter. *I like this kid,* he decided. "C'mon." He waved at Chad to follow. Together they made their way over piles of old diggings and down the creek bank. "There's a dirty sock in your coffee," Jem remarked when Strike grasped the cup.

"Yep." Strike took a swallow and turned back to his rocker.

Jem and Chad exchanged amused looks.

"Who's your friend?" Strike asked, peering at Chad from under his slouch hat. His hand continued to rock the cradle. Gravel rattled and bounced around on the screen.

"Chad Carter," Jem said. "I just met him, so I don't know where he's from or what he's doing here. Chad, this is Strike-it-rich Sam, a friend and my partner. We sometimes prospect together."

Strike pierced Chad with a keen look. "Carter, eh?" He stopped working his rocker and reached for a beat-up gold pan. "You reckon your pa and Sterling will get the mine up and runnin' again?"

Chad shrugged. "I reckon they'll do their best."

Jem's thoughts whirled. This new kid was the other mine owner's son? How did Strike know that? *Dumb question.* Strike-it-rich Sam wandered up and down the gold fields, all his worldly possessions piled on Canary's back. He scraped together a meager living and kept to himself. But behind the miner's odd ways and scruffy appearance lay a mind as quick as a steel trap. Of *course* he would know who owned what in Goldtown.

Strike grunted his opinion of Chad's answer and splashed his way into the creek to pan what the rocker had separated.

Jem let him go without offering to help. If Strike wanted to wear himself out working his pan one-handed, then Jem would let him. A few more weeks in the splint, and his partner's arm would be good as new. *Maybe Strike's cussedness will disappear too, and he'll be back to his cheerful self.*

Jem hoped so. He turned his back on Strike and motioned Chad over to where Jem's gold pan lay abandoned. By now, Nathan and Ellie had tired of their water fight. They sat resting at the edge of the creek.

Before Ellie could open her mouth, Jem introduced the new boy. "He's the other mine owner's son," he finished.

"Are you as rich as the Sterlings?" Ellie blurted.

Jem gasped. "*Ellie!*"

"Richer," Chad teased, plopping to the ground.

"Pay her no mind," Jem muttered.

Chad burst out laughing at Ellie's round eyes and red cheeks. "I've got a sister your age," he told her. "Wish Father had brought her. You and Kate would get along like bread and butter. She's mouthy too."

Ellie pressed her lips together, snatched up her gold pan, and stomped back into the creek.

Jem felt a sliver of guilt for letting the new boy tease Ellie, but *roasted rattlesnakes!* Why would she ask such a rude question? He flicked a glance at Nathan, warning him to keep any personal questions to himself. Nathan shrugged his understanding.

"Does she really pan for gold?" Chad asked, staring at Ellie. She was knee deep in the creek, working her pan around and around.

"What? Oh, yeah. She's pretty good." Jem dug into his pocket and drew out his leather pouch. "Look." He loosened the strings and emptied the contents into his free hand. "This is what I've panned so far this year. It's not much, but—"

Chad whistled, and his blue eyes gleamed. "It looks like a lot to *me*." Then he sighed. "Owning a mine isn't the same as panning for gold with your own two hands." He picked up Jem's largest nugget. "Is it yours? I mean, do you get to keep what you find?"

"Of course!"

"Lucky. I wish . . ." Chad's voice trailed off. He dropped the nugget into Jem's hand and shrugged.

Jem returned the gold to his pouch and stuffed it back in his pocket. Did this rich boy wish he could get his hands dirty panning for gold in an icy creek? It didn't make sense. Will Sterling wouldn't be caught dead digging in the mud and gravel for a gold flake—not when his father owned a mine full of gold. *Correction*, Jem reminded himself. *It used to be full of gold.*

Chad Carter seemed different. Jem wondered what he was doing out here. It was a long walk—or ride—from Belle Hill to Cripple Creek. What had lured Chad away from his hosts?

Suddenly, Jem knew. The Sterling hospitality had most likely worn off, and Will's annoying ways had sent Chad running in the other direction—*any* direction. Chad was probably used to riding far and wide on his ranch. Being stuffed into a fancy mansion would suffocate anyone, rich or poor.

"Listen, Chad," Jem offered. "If you'd like to try your hand panning for gold, you can use my pan. I'll show you a trick or two."

Chad snatched up the gold pan that lay at his feet. "What are we waiting for? I'd be happy to find anything . . . any little flake will do." He paused. "Is it hard to learn?"

"Depends."

"If Jem can teach a greenhorn from Boston how to pan gold," Nathan put in, "then he can surely teach a cowboy from the Valley."

Jem grinned at his cousin's words. "Nathan's right, Chad. I'll have you panning for gold in no time."

⚔ CHAPTER 7 ⚔

Gold Fever

It took Jem a few minutes to find just the right spot in the creek alongside the Coulter gold claim. It took another minute to shoo Ellie and Nathan away. "One teacher is all Chad needs," Jem decided. "You'll just muddy the water and get in the way."

Ellie scooted out of the creek, plopped down on a rock, and hiked her knees under her skirt until just her bare toes poked out. She rested her chin on her knees and sat perfectly still.

Like a hungry coyote eyeing a field mouse, Jem thought with a frown. "Hang it all, Ellie!" he shouted from where he and Chad stood in the creek barely a stone's throw away. "You don't need to watch."

"I'm not watching," Ellie yelled back. "I'm drying out. Nathan soaked me, and I'm cold." She pushed a shirt sleeve up past her elbow. "See? Goose bumps up and down my arm."

"I'm not watching either," Nathan said. He sat down next to Ellie, pulled his knees up, and grinned.

From the nearby claim, Strike let out a hoot of laughter before going back to his own business. "Yes sirree, Jem," he cackled, "you got your hands full today."

"Don't pay 'em no mind," Jem told his new friend. "They're like a couple of fussy ol' schoolmarms. Soon as they see you do something wrong, they'll leap up and holler at you to do it their way."

Chad laughed. "Let 'em holler all they want. I'm used to it. I have an older brother, a younger one, and two little sisters."

Jem took the gold pan from Chad. Dipping it in the stream, he brought up a mixture of gravel, sand, and water. "You pick out the big rocks and pitch 'em back in the creek," he instructed. "Then you swirl the pan around, add more water, and wash the sand and little chunks out. The heavier gold stays at the bottom of the pan—so long as you don't go too fast and wash the gold out too."

"That's it?" Chad asked. He looked eager to begin.

"It's not as easy as it looks," Ellie called from the creek bank. "Jem, don't forget to tell him—"

"Ellie!"

Ellie huffed and shot to her feet. Stumbling over the sharp rocks and mounds of old diggings, she clambered up the creek bank and out of sight. A sudden, ornery-sounding *hee-haw* told Jem his sister had taken her complaints to Canary.

Good riddance. Now, maybe we can pan in peace.

Jem turned back to Chad and handed him the full gold pan. "Ellie's right," he admitted. "It's not easy. And it takes a lot of time. *Hours* sometimes. There isn't near the gold in Cripple Creek like there used to be. In the old days, miners could reach down"—he scooped up a handful of dripping sand and gravel—"and pick up a fistful of gold nuggets. But not anymore."

Slowly, Jem opened his hand and let the dirt and rocks splash back into the creek. *No gold in the creek. No gold in the mine.* "Anyway, you have to be patient," he said, shaking himself free from his gloomy thoughts.

Chad squatted and started working his pan. "My brother

Justin's the patient one in my family. I'm the quick one. But when I get fired up about something, I can do what it takes. And I'm fired up about finding some gold of my own."

There seemed to be no stopping the new kid from searching for what little gold might be at his feet. Pan after empty pan, Chad did not give up. An hour dragged by before Jem finally pointed out three shiny specks no bigger than pinheads. They sparkled along the edge of his pan.

Chad's eyes lit up, but when he tried to pick up the small particles, he lost them. "Doggone it! They're too tiny to hang on to."

"You've done pretty good for a first try," Jem said. He glanced up at the sun. The day was getting away from them. Ellie was still out of sight. Nathan had lost interest in the lesson and wandered over to watch Strike-it-rich Sam and his rocker. "You can come back tomorrow if you want."

"I'm just getting the hang of it," Chad protested. "One more try? I'm in no hurry to go back to the Sterlings."

Jem didn't doubt that. "How long have you and your pa been in town?"

"*Too* long. Four or five days. I've lost count. Father brought me along so I could learn the mining business." Chad cringed. "He should've brought Justin instead. He's gonna be a lawyer some day, so he likes that sort of thing. Me? I just want to ranch. I don't care about anything else. But Mother figures different, I reckon. She wants me to 'widen my horizons,' whatever *that* means."

Chad scooped up another pan of gravel and grit, then sighed. "I got tired of being a polite guest. I couldn't sit still any longer, listening to dull talk about mines, stamp mills, and surveys." He shrugged. "So, I saddled a horse and took off."

Jem squatted beside Chad, heart pounding. *He listened in on mining meetings?* Maybe Chad knew what was going on with the Midas mine. Had the men been paid? Were they still rioting? Had a new vein of gold been surveyed? Would the miners go back to work? Could Goldtown be saved?

Questions tumbled around inside Jem's head, clawing to get out. He knew only what Will had told him last week. Pa didn't say much either. But he was gone more than he was home, so Jem knew some kind of trouble was still brewing.

He studied the boy working steadily at his side. Chad might be a possible source of news, and he was much friend-lier than Will. "Can you pan for gold and talk at the same time?" he asked.

Chad paused. "Yeah, why?"

Jem pointed to the side of his head. Every morning, the cracked mirror in his attic loft showed Jem that his face was still bruised and swollen. But it was no longer painful, and he felt fine. "I got caught in a riot the other day. The miners were demanding their pay. They broke down the office to look for it."

"I thought a horse kicked you," Chad said, grinning. "So what?"

"So, I want to know what's going on. Will told me only a little bit, and I had to lose a checkers game just to get him to talk."

Chad laughed. "Bet that was hard to do. He's terrible at checkers." He swirled his pan a couple more times and picked out a few small rocks. "What do you want to know?"

Jem took a deep breath and thought about which ques-tion he wanted to ask first. He settled on the most impor-tant one. "Is the Midas mine going to close down for good? I mean . . . if it does, Goldtown will turn into a ghost town. It's not much of a town, but it's my home. I don't want to see it vanish like other gold camps."

"I'm not sure," Chad said, "but there's talk that the survey discovered another vein."

Jem's heart soared. *Thank you, God!* As long as the miners knew they would eventually go back to work, they might not riot again. Perhaps the mine owners would give them a portion of their pay in advance, just to tide them over until the blasting opened up the new vein. Things would return to normal. Jem could visit town. His frog-leg business had dried up the past week, but now he could make deliveries again. *Mr. Sims at the café will be happy to hear that.*

Jem's excitement spilled over. "How long 'til the mine reopens?"

"Simmer down," Chad said. "I have no idea. I don't even know if it *will* reopen."

"But you just said—"

"Wait." Chad paused in his panning, peered at the silt, and blew out a disappointed breath. Then he rinsed his pan and started over. "They found a new vein, but I hear it goes real deep."

"That's good, right? It means there's lots of gold in your mine."

Chad shrugged. "I suppose. But blasting so far underground means they'll need a new air shaft. Otherwise, the miners suffocate down there."

Jem sat still, pondering. If it meant being able to reach the gold, it was worth digging an air shaft. What was the problem? "So, dig an air shaft. It'll take time, but the mine will reopen. That's the important thing."

"I thought so too," Chad agreed. He put down the pan and looked at Jem. "Father and Mr. Sterling seem to think it's more complicated than just making an air shaft." He pointed up. "The shaft needs to stretch from the lower mine to the surface. It will go right through another, older mine that sits above the Midas. Mr. Sterling says he has to reclaim that mine."

Jem's ears pricked up. He tried to visualize what might

be resting on top of an important mine like the Midas, but nothing came to mind. He shook his head. "I don't know of any other mines."

"This one's really old," Chad said. "It used to belong to Mr. Sterling. He calls it the"—he wrinkled his forehead—"let's see . . . the Belle."

Jem jumped up. Water splashed in Chad's face. He yelped and dropped the gold pan. It headed downstream.

"What are you so fired up about?" Chad demanded, sloshing after the pan. With a quick swipe, he rescued it and rounded on Jem.

"The Belle isn't much of a mine," Jem answered. "Just a tunnel that barely scratches the surface. I don't think it goes more than a hundred yards or so into the hill."

"So, you do know it."

Jem nodded. "Those diggings have been abandoned for years. Once the easy gold played out, nobody wanted to work it anymore."

"It won't be hard to reclaim it then, and use it for part of the air shaft."

Jem shook his head. "You don't understand, Chad. Once a claim is abandoned, scavengers can take over. It's hard work once the easy gold is gone, but they do it."

"Huh?" Chad's eyebrows rose. "I've heard of scavenger birds, like buzzards. But scavenger *people?*"

"They're folks who work claims after the miners move on."

"What's this got to do with the Belle?"

"People are working the Belle diggings right now," Jem said. "They've got scavenger rights on the claim. As long as they pay their foreign miner's tax every month, they have a legal right to work it."

"Foreign miner's tax?" Chad looked puzzled.

"Yeah. They're Chinese. My friend Wu Shen and his relatives work that claim." Jem took a deep breath. "And I betcha all the gold in California they won't let anybody reclaim their mine for any ol' air shaft."

"That's rather hard luck for Mr. Sterling and Father," Chad said. "Not to mention for the entire town."

Jem slumped. A sudden breeze made him shiver, in spite of the hot afternoon sun. Chad was right. Hard luck indeed!

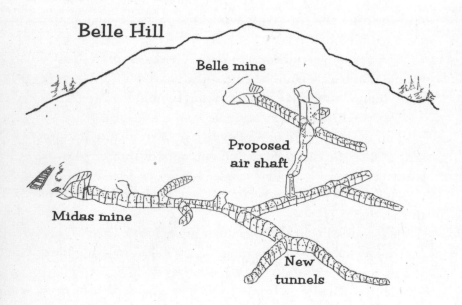

⚔ CHAPTER 8 ⚔

Branding Irons

When Chad gave a shout of surprise ten minutes later, Jem's thoughts were a thousand miles away. He stood idly by, watching Strike dump yet another bucket of creek water through his rocker screen. Jem could have snagged Ellie's gold pan and worked some gravel, but he didn't. He was too busy thinking about Wu Shen, the air shaft, and the old Belle diggings.

Chad's "Is it gold?" jerked Jem's attention back to his friend. The boy's eyes gleamed—just like Nathan's when he'd found his first bit of color. Chad shoved the pan under Jem's nose. "Is it?"

One quick look told Jem the story. *Fool's gold.* The sparkling chunk stood out from the rest of the pebbles, sand particles, and silt in Chad's pan. Gold might still be buried under the mud, but this big, shiny rock was not the pure stuff. Chad looked so eager—so excited. *How do I tell him the bad news?*

Then Jem's hand went to his pocket. He fingered his pouch, loosened the strings, and felt around for one of the larger nuggets. "Let me have a closer look," he said. With his free hand, he lifted the fool's gold and eyed it carefully.

Chad held his breath.

"I'm sorry, Chad, but it's fool's gold," Jem said finally. He tossed it back in the creek.

Chad whirled and dropped the pan. "Hey! Are you sure? Why did you throw it away?"

Jem rescued the gold pan just in time. "Fool's gold is worthless. But don't give up. Finish panning the rest of this muck."

Scowling, Chad crouched and began to slosh around what was left in his pan.

"Slow down," Jem warned. *Or I will have just wasted a perfectly good gold nugget.* "Look!"

Chad peered into the pan and caught his breath. "Is that gold?"

"Yep. *That* is gold." Jem picked up the pea-sized nugget and smiled. "Not bad, Chad. Not bad at all."

"Yippee!" Chad snatched the gold from Jem and held it up. "Just wait 'til my brothers see this beauty! They'll turn green as pea soup." He slapped Jem on the back. "You *are* a good teacher."

His shouts brought Ellie and Nathan running. Puffing out his chest, Chad showed off his gold. Even Strike-it-rich Sam took a few minutes to admire it. After all, a fella's first strike was something special—even if he *did* have a little help.

When the gold was safely stashed in Chad's pocket, Jem gathered up their pans and shovels and dumped them near Strike's campfire. "Keep an eye on our tools, will ya?" he called to the old prospector. "We're heading home."

Strike waved. "Tell your pa howdy," he called in farewell.

"Do you need a ride?" Jem asked Chad as they picked their way across the old, abandoned gold claims and headed to the tree line. "Copper can carry four as easily as three. We can drop you off at the bottom of Belle Hill."

"I told you I rode out," Chad replied. He pointed beneath a scrub oak. "There's my horse."

Jem's mouth dropped open. There was no mistaking the paint horse's markings. "That . . . that's . . ."

"That's Will's horse!" Ellie finished with a gasp. "He doesn't let anybody ride Prince Charming. Not *anybody*." She gaped at Chad, her hazel eyes round with respect. "How didja get him to—"

"I didn't ask him. Mr. Sterling told Father we could borrow their horses. I picked a likely-looking one and saddled him up." Chad shoved his hat farther down over his eyes and chewed on his lip. "Maybe Will won't notice he's gone."

"He'd have to be blind as a post hole not to notice his best horse is missing," Jem said, laughing. "Boy, are you ever gonna get it when you get back."

"Then I just won't go back yet," Chad said, hurrying to the paint horse. He untied him and followed Jem to the chestnut gelding tied up fifty yards away. "How 'bout showing me your place? Do you live in town? I mean, since your father's the sheriff an' all."

Jem hesitated. "We . . . we have a small ranch a couple miles out of town."

Chad's eyes lit up. "How many cattle do you run?"

"Uh . . . a couple dozen or so, plus calves." He didn't ask Chad how many cattle *his* family owned. They probably had so many they couldn't be counted—all fat, sleek, and well-fed on rich alfalfa hay.

"That's a good start," Chad said. He didn't offer to share—or boast—about their own numbers, and Jem relaxed. "Why don't you ride out with me?" Chad added. "I'd like to see your spread."

Jem, Ellie, and Nathan exchanged worried looks. Jem remembered Nathan's words when he first saw the ranch: *No amount of chores can fix this place up.* If a city cousin from back

East thought the Coulter ranch was a dump, what would a rich rancher's kid think? Jem swallowed. There was no easy way out of this fix.

Chad climbed in the saddle and offered Jem his hand. "Mount up. I'm sure Prince *Charming*"—he chuckled—"can carry us both."

The chance to hitch a ride on Will's precious horse was too much for Jem to refuse. It was even worth letting Chad see the rundown Coulter spread. Grinning, he handed Copper's reins to Ellie. "See you back at the ranch." Then he grasped Chad's hand and clambered up behind his new friend.

"Will's gonna have a conniption fit when he finds out you rode his horse!" Ellie shouted after them, but Jem just laughed.

A few minutes later, Chad cut through town. Jem's conscience flickered. The streets were quiet this afternoon, but Jem did not want to linger. Pa might step out of his sheriff's office just as Jem rode by. It would be awkward trying to explain why he was trotting through town with a strange boy on the Sterlings' horse.

"Can we go a little faster?" he urged Chad. He craned his neck as they passed the jailhouse.

"Sure!" Prince Charming broke into a swinging lope at Chad's command.

Jem had often watched Will try to manage his horse. The paint fought the bit and caused all sorts of trouble. Today, however, he did everything his rider asked. It was easy to see that the Carter boy knew his way around horses.

"Turn here," Jem directed.

"How does your father find time to run a ranch and be a sheriff too?" Chad asked when they'd rounded the corner and left Goldtown behind. The road to the ranch wound between hills covered with scrub oaks and pines and through summer-dry creek beds.

Jem wanted to say that Pa could do anything and every-thing, and do it well. But the hard truth of the last couple of months—and especially the past week—told a different tale. "He was keeping up pretty well," Jem said, "until this trouble with the mine broke out. Now he's never home. I've got heaps of chores, but my aunt let me off easy until my head healed."

He let out a long, disappointed sigh. "Not a lot is get-ting done. Our calves haven't even been branded yet, and a couple of fences are getting ready to fall over."

Chad slowed Prince Charming to a walk and turned around in the saddle to look at Jem. "I don't know how long Father plans to stay in Goldtown. Probably until he and Mr. Sterling get the mine reopened."

"That won't happen if they need an air shaft," Jem muttered.

"Maybe not, but Father will think of something," Chad said. "We might be here a couple more weeks. I know lots about running a ranch." He gave Jem a wide smile. "I know how to brand calves. I could teach you."

"Pa was going to teach me," Jem said, "but he never got around to it. Who knows how long it'll be put off now?"

"I can mend fences too." Chad made a face. "It's not my favorite chore, so I know how to get it done fast."

Better and better! "It would sure take a load off Pa's mind if I could help out more," Jem said. "When do you want to start?"

"Depends. How many calves have you got?" Chad asked.

"Just a handful so far—eight or nine."

The boys trotted through the broken gate and up the short drive. Jem motioned Chad to stop near the barn, then he slid off the paint horse and looked around. Ellie and Nathan were nowhere in sight. They must have gone the long way, clear around the outskirts of Goldtown. It meant

Nathan had the reins. Ellie would have raced Jem through town to get home first.

Chad tied Prince Charming to an old post. "We could brand a couple of calves every day 'til the job gets done. I suppose they're roaming all over the place?" His face showed that he hoped they were. When Jem nodded, he grinned. "Let's get to it."

"Right now?"

"Sure!"

Caught up in Chad's excitement, Jem rummaged around in the barn until he found the JE branding iron. "Pa used Ellie's and my initials for the brand," he explained. He dug out a coil of rope and an extra pair of leather gloves for Chad and found his saddle. "Soon as Ellie and Nathan get back, I'll saddle Copper up."

Chad nodded. "They'll need to help too. Branding is a three- or four-person job. It takes a lot to hold down an ornery critter while somebody brands it."

"You're the boss," Jem said, grinning. "Thanks for doing this."

"Fair's fair," Chad said. He whipped his gold nugget from his pocket and held it up. "You taught me to pan for gold. I can teach you to brand a calf."

A few minutes later, Ellie and Nathan trotted into the yard. If Ellie was surprised to see Jem holding the branding iron, she didn't let on. Without a word, she slid from Copper's back and watched Jem toss a blanket and saddle over his horse.

"Does Uncle Matthew know what you're up to?" Nathan asked when Jem told Ellie to whistle for Quicksilver. He chewed on his lip and scuffed the dirt. "Seems to me that branding calves is a job for grown-ups. It sounds dangerous. I'm sure Mother would not—"

"Pa never said we couldn't brand calves," Jem said, cinching his saddle tight. If his cousin spoiled their surprise by squealing to Aunt Rose, he'd . . . well . . . he'd find the biggest king snake in the hills and hide it in Nathan's bed. "You know he was gonna teach us." He turned to Chad. "How many calves have you helped brand?"

Chad looped a lasso around Prince Charming's saddle horn. "This spring? Hundreds, maybe more. I lost count." He looked Nathan up and down. "You don't *look* like a city-raised greenhorn, but you sure talk like one. Are you game enough to give us a hand with the branding?"

"I am," Ellie said, leading the dapple-gray horse over to the boys. "I betcha branding a calf is no more work than standing for hours in an icy-cold stream lookin' for gold." She peered at Chad. "Betcha I can brand a calf better than your sister, whatever-her-name-is."

Chad grinned and yanked one of Ellie's auburn braids. "Her name's Kate, and we'll *see* if you can do better."

"I'm game," Nathan agreed. He sounded only a little hesitant.

By the time they gathered their supplies and left the yard, the sun had dipped lower in the late afternoon sky. Jem gave his friend a worried look.

"We've got plenty of time," Chad replied to Jem's unspoken question.

It didn't take long to find a small group of cows and calves. The mothers lay in the shade beneath a large, spreading oak tree, chewing their cud. Four calves frisked about. Jem kindled a small, hot fire and set the branding iron in the middle of it.

"Do you want to go after the calf or should I?" Chad asked, fingering his lasso.

From the look in his eyes, Jem knew Chad was eager to show off his roping skills. It was just as well. Jem could find every last bit of gold dust in a bucket of dirt, but what he knew about roping a calf would not fill Aunt Rose's thimble. "You go on," he said, before Ellie blurted the truth.

Chad grinned and loosened his rope. "I'll rope him and drag him to the fire. As long as this fancy horse will stand still and hold the calf, we can catch him and throw him down. Easy as pie."

Chad not only made it sound easy, he made it look easy as well. Before the cows could guess what was happening, he had maneuvered Prince Charming between one of the calves and its mama. The chase was on, but it was short-lived. On his first throw, Chad's lasso sailed through the air and settled neatly around the calf's neck. Chad jerked, and the rope tightened. He dallied the other end around his saddle horn and headed back.

"He's good," Ellie breathed in awe.

Jem didn't answer. His mouth was hanging open.

By the time Chad dragged the protesting calf to the fire, Jem had managed to shut his mouth. But his heart gave a sudden skip. The calf looked a lot bigger up close than it did from a distance. Worse, the agitated bawling of Mama cow was getting louder—and closer.

"Hurry!" Chad waved Jem and Nathan over. Ellie had been chosen to do the actual branding. She stood by the fire, waiting for her cue.

The three boys wrestled the calf to the ground.

Ooof! Jem grunted when he hit the dirt. This was no one-week-old baby, but a much older, strong and healthy bull calf. Pa could have slapped him to the ground in a heartbeat, but Jem had all he could do to hold his own against the terrified animal. He was so busy trying to keep his share of the calf down that he barely heard Chad yell at Ellie.

Jem looked up to see Ellie standing over them, the handle of the red-hot iron clutched tightly in her hand. "What are you waiting for?" he sputtered. "Brand him!"

Too late. The cow's angry bellows spurred the calf into one last frenzy to escape. A hind leg darted out and caught Jem in the thigh. The pain loosened his grip. Taking advantage of his partial freedom, the calf kicked harder. Nathan howled and fell away. Ellie shrieked, dropped the iron, and ran.

Jem heard sizzling and smelled burnt cloth. The next moment he felt the searing heat of the branding iron against his flailing arm.

⊰ CHAPTER 9 ⊱

Aftermath

The branding iron touched Jem's flesh for no more than a second, but the pain sent him scuttling away from the red-hot metal. His eyes watered, and he clenched his teeth to keep from yelping. His breath came in quick gasps. The shock of nearly being branded scared him as much as the stinging burn. He felt sudden compassion for the calf.

Chad sat a few feet away, dangling the now-empty rope from his hand. "I freed him just in time. Mama was headed for us at stampede speed." He let out a long, shuddering breath. "I guess he was too much calf for us."

Good guess, Chad! But a little late. Through watering eyes, Jem watched the calf kick up his heels and rejoin his mother. They headed back to the trees as if nothing had happened.

Nothing *had* happened . . . to the calf. Jem's arm, however, throbbed.

Chad reached out and slipped a finger through the burnt edges of Jem's shirt sleeve. "Looks like the wrong target got the brand." He wasn't smiling. "Bet it hurts like blazes."

Jem glanced at his arm and winced. "It does." He cracked a smile—a small one—to show Chad he could take it. "It coulda been worse. You might not have freed the calf in time.

Being trampled by the cow would make my burn look like nothin'."

"You're right about that," Chad agreed with a sober nod. "God gave my fingers extra speed, 'cause I was doin' a lot of prayin' right about then."

"So was I," Ellie piped up. She stood above Jem. Her tear-filled eyes looked huge and scared. "I'm sorry I dropped the iron on you, Jem." Tears dripped down her cheeks, but she rubbed them away. "I saw that ol' cow coming, and I just ran."

Jem reached up and squeezed Ellie's hand. "I'm glad you did. Can you imagine what Pa would do to me if that cow had trampled you?" He laughed. "You saved your own skin, and mine besides."

Ellie managed a watery smile. "When you look at it that way, I reckon I did make the right choice."

Jem looked around for the last member of their ill-fated branding team. Nathan sat just beyond Chad, with his knees bent and his head down—still as a statue. "Are you hurt?" Jem asked.

Nathan shook his head but didn't look up. He mumbled something Jem couldn't catch.

"What did you say?"

Nathan raised his head. His face was white. Two red spots flamed his cheeks. "I said, 'I told you it was dangerous.'"

Jem said nothing. Neither did Chad. For another minute they sat silently, staring at the ground. Finally, Jem pulled himself to his feet and glanced at the sinking sun. "We better get home." He took a step and winced. His right thigh ached from the kick the calf had given him; his left arm stung. "Do cowboys always hurt like this?" he asked Chad, who had risen with him.

"Yep."

Jem limped to the fire. It had burned down to coals. He scooped up handfuls of dirt and buried what remained of the embers. Chad and Ellie helped. Dust rose in clouds. Coughing and sneezing, Jem made his way to Copper. Nathan stirred and joined Ellie on Quicksilver.

The quiet group rode their horses off the range and back to the yard. The surprise Jem wanted to give his father had turned into a near-disaster. True, Chad was an expert roper. He clearly knew how to throw a calf and hold it down. But someone should have been on horseback, keeping the cow away from her calf. Why had no one thought of that? Jem shivered at their close call.

"Maybe Pa isn't home yet," he said, mostly to himself.

For once, Jem hoped Pa's sheriff duties had kept him in town long enough so Jem could put away the evidence of their failed branding attempt. He didn't want his father to worry over what had happened. Pa had enough on his mind trying to keep order in town with the out-of-work miners.

"Maybe he'll say, 'All's well that ends well,'" Ellie said brightly. Now that the trouble was over, she seemed back to her carefree self. Jem envied her. He wished he could be as easygoing. "Nobody got hurt too bad," she added. "Pa will figure we learned our lesson."

I sure have, Jem told God in a quick prayer. *I learned to stay far away from the working end of a hot branding iron. Next time, Pa can hold down the calf and I'll do the branding.*

If there was a next time. *Please, God, let there be a next time!*

By the time Jem rode Copper around to the front of the barn, his arm was screaming for attention. He wanted a cold cloth, ice from the icebox, a stream of water from the pump—anything to cool his injury and give him relief. Next to his burn, the bruise on his thigh faded to a minor annoyance.

"Look!" The catch in Ellie's voice pulled Jem from his injuries and back to his surroundings. Three riders were coming up the driveway.

"Uh-oh," Chad murmured.

Jem recognized two of the riders—Pa and Mr. Sterling. The other was a man Jem didn't know. And . . . *Uh-oh is right!* Will sat behind his father on the large bay horse. He looked madder than a peeled rattler.

Chad and Jem exchanged uneasy looks. Then Chad sat up straighter in his saddle. Jem wanted to give Copper a kick and hightail it into the hills, but he sat up straight too. He gripped Copper's reins and swallowed his panic. The branding iron hung in plain sight, tied to his saddle. It was still warm. If Pa touched it—

"Off the horses!" Pa ordered when he came within shouting range. His face was dark with either anger or frustration. Jem didn't know which, but it didn't matter. He flew off Copper faster even than Chad. Ellie and Nathan slipped and slid from Quicksilver's back as one, landing on their backsides with a *thunk*.

Pa's shout brought Aunt Rose running from the garden on the other side of the house. Her arms were full of carrots, and her straw sunhat flapped as she ran. "Why on earth are you shouting, Matthew?" Then she saw the boys and Ellie. "Oh, my! I didn't realize you were home. Who is your friend?"

Jem didn't answer. Neither did Nathan or Ellie.

Pa dismounted, walked over to Jem, and looked the horses over. His eyes focused on the branding iron, ropes, and other gear hanging from their mounts. He shook his head. "What tomfool notion has got into you, boy? Surely you're not thinking of branding a calf!"

The stranger stepped up just then, saving Jem from answering. *This must be Chad's father.* He had the same black hair and blue eyes, and he was regarding Chad with the exact same look Pa was giving Jem.

"You've been accused of being a horse thief, Son," Mr. Carter said in a deep, no-nonsense voice. "That's a serious charge." He said nothing about the branding tools.

Chad ducked his head and stared at his boots.

Will dismounted from his father's horse. He ran up to Chad and pointed an accusing finger at him. "I went to the barn and found my horse missing. I thought he'd been stolen. Of *course* Father had to report it to the sheriff. How was I supposed to know you took him?"

Jem shot Will a furious glare. "You could have taken a good guess."

Pa crossed his arms. "Nine Toes saw the two of you parading through town earlier on the 'stolen' horse," he said. "He figured you were headed this way. I'd already spent a good part of the afternoon—time I could have spent here at home—trying to help the Sterlings recover Prince Charming."

Jem suddenly wished he'd ridden Copper home from the creek with Ellie and Nathan. "I didn't take Will's horse," he insisted. "I just hitched a ride."

Pa dropped his arms to his sides and let out a breath. "So, Ernest, the horse has been found. Do you intend to press charges against this young man?" He nodded at Chad, whose head had snapped up at the question.

Mr. Sterling's eyebrows rose. "Of course not, Sheriff. I did, after all, open my stables to my guests. It just never occurred to me that my young visitor would take a horse and disappear without telling anyone."

"He does that a lot," Mr. Carter put in. He wasn't smiling, but a twinkle came to his eyes.

"*I* want to press charges, Sheriff Coulter," Will said. He stood next to Prince Charming, his face a dark scowl. "Look at my horse. He's sweaty and filthy. Mistreated and probably ridden into the ground. At the least, I insist that—"

"Chad will curry and care for your horse, Will," Mr. Carter assured him. Before Will could reply, the tall rancher turned to Pa. "My son has the makings of a good rancher, but he falls a bit short when it comes to thinking things through. He gets fired up about something and *bang*—like a pistol shot—he's off."

He waved a hand toward the branding gear tied to Copper's saddle. "Thank the Good Lord we caught these youngsters before they really got themselves into a fix."

Jem sucked in his breath and glanced at Chad. *They don't know!* Chad gave him a tiny nod of understanding. Overwhelmed by his good fortune, Jem relaxed. Will's dirty looks slid off him like water over rocks. He smiled, in spite of his burning arm. "You have a good horse, Will."

Jem meant it. Prince Charming had stood his ground like a true cow pony today, only . . . Will might not like to know what his precious horse had been used for.

Will's scowl lightened at Jem's words. He grunted a curt thanks and mounted the paint horse. Then Mr. Carter motioned Chad to join him on his horse. Mr. Sterling thanked Pa for his help, and the ranch visitors disappeared down the drive.

Jem, Ellie, and Nathan watched them leave without a word. Aunt Rose, who had been silent the entire time, suddenly asked, "What have you three been up to?"

"Nothing!" The word exploded from them at the same time.

Jem flinched and looked at Pa. His father stood by quietly, but his eyes were busy flicking from Jem to Copper, and back to Jem again. His gaze rested on Jem's scorched shirt sleeve, and his brow wrinkled.

Aunt Rose tapped her foot against the ground. Dust puffed out from beneath her long skirt. "You're as jumpy as frogs on a hot griddle," she accused them. "Might as well come clean."

Suddenly, Pa walked over and wrapped an arm around his sister's shoulder. "Rosie, the sun's going down, and those carrots are wilting in this heat. Why don't you take Ellie and Nathan inside to help with supper? I'll give Jem a hand putting up the horses."

Aunt Rose gave Pa a questioning look then turned and herded Ellie and Nathan toward the house.

"Come on, Jem," Pa said when the yard was empty, "we need to talk."

⇥ CHAPTER 10 ⇤

Scavengers and Miners

Jem groaned. He snatched Copper's reins and followed Pa and Quicksilver into the barn to put away the branding equipment and unsaddle his horse. Pa took care of the dappled horse without speaking. When he turned Quicksilver out to pasture and returned to the barn, Jem was still struggling with his saddle.

"It's hard to care for a horse with only one good arm," Pa remarked. He reached around Jem, lifted the heavy saddle from Copper, and put it away.

Jem nodded in defeat. His arm felt like it was still on fire, branding his flesh all over again. *Why did a burn hurt so much?*

Gently, Pa reached his finger through the blackened edges of Jem's shirt sleeve and ripped it away. Jem looked down and gasped. Part of an angry-red J glared up at him from just above his elbow. Bits of the E showed as well. The burn was already blistering.

Pa shook his head. "I reckon there's not much left to say except I'm glad it's not worse. And I don't mean your new 'brand.' You might've started a wildfire and burned down the range, not to mention—"

"Pa!" Jem interrupted. "I was extra careful with the fire.

And Chad was there. He's branded hundreds and hundreds of calves. Everything was going fine until . . ." He paused at the disappointed look on Pa's face and ducked his head. "I'm sorry. I wanted to help out with the ranch chores more, on account of you've got so much going on with the miners and Mr. Sterling, and . . ." His voice trailed off.

"I'm not faulting you for your good intentions, Jem," Pa said. "But even the best intentions need a bit of common sense. Your aunt let you off chores this week because you got thumped on the head. So"—Pa let out a weary breath—"what do you do? You take on something that's more work than all your other ranch chores put together."

Jem had no answer. He apologized again and hoped the scolding was over. It appeared to be, until Pa said, "Rose is still having a hard time adjusting to life out here. I just got her convinced that rattlesnakes don't sneak up through the floorboards and the cattle won't stampede across the yard."

Pa led Copper out of the barn. Jem stayed on his heels. "And it took all my sweet-talking to convince her that you youngsters are in no danger roaming free," Pa finished with another sigh. He stopped and turned to look at Jem. "It might be best to spare your aunt the worry of this latest incident. I'm not sure how she'd take it if she knew."

"Yes, sir," Jem agreed wholeheartedly.

"If Chad and his father want to lend a hand with my scrawny calves, I won't say no," Pa said. He jabbed a finger in Jem's chest. "But no more branding on your own." He didn't wait for a reply but headed toward the field to turn Copper loose.

"Thanks, Pa," Jem whispered at his father's back.

It was the mildest rebuke Jem had ever received. The scolding Pa had given Ellie and him when they played hooky from school had packed more punch than this. Jem knew why. Angry words or even a well-deserved licking couldn't hold a candle to the price Jem had already paid for this lesson.

Jem stopped by the pump and cooled his arm under a slow trickle. It didn't help much. Then he ducked through the back door, hoping to sneak up the ladder and into the attic for a clean shirt. He didn't dare sit down to supper in these rags. Aunt Rose had the eyes of a—

"Jeremiah Isaiah, what on earth happened to your shirt? It's missing one entire sl—" Her voice caught. "Land sakes alive, child!" In a flash, Aunt Rose was at Jem's side, sputtering like Miss Cluck, Ellie's favorite setting hen. "I need to tend that burn at once. Goodness knows how this happened, but I'll have you fixed up in no time."

To Jem's astonishment, tears came to Aunt Rose's eyes as she ushered him into a straight-back chair and told him to stay put. Then she scurried away.

Nathan and Ellie crowded around Jem, eyes huge at the letter branded into Jem's arm.

"Will you have a permanent mark?" Ellie asked.

Before Jem could answer, Aunt Rose was back with her basket of herbs and potions. She cleaned and dressed Jem's burn while she scolded him up one side and down the other about his carelessness with fire. Then she blamed "that filthy prospector you hobnob with" for letting Jem go too near his campfire.

Jem kept quiet and let Aunt Rose fuss all she wanted. Strike-it-rich Sam was already low down on Aunt Rose's ladder of respectable folks. It wouldn't bother the old miner to learn he'd just been booted to the bottom rung. Jem saw Pa standing in the doorway, arms crossed over his chest, grinning like a Cheshire cat.

Jem smiled back.

Supper was served late that night. Pa gave an extra-long blessing over the food. Trouble was, Pa talked to the Lord more about instilling good judgment in his children than thanking Him for the steaming kettle of chicken and dumplings. Jem's stomach rumbled. *Pa is preaching, not praying.*

Jem's "amen" came out in a breath of relief. Aunt Rose shot him a sharp look before passing him a heaping plate of food. Jem gave her an innocent smile and dug into his meal. Preaching or praying, it did feel good to see Pa sitting at the table for once. This whole week had been worse than the town burning down, in Jem's opinion. Towns could be rebuilt. Empty mines could not be reclaimed.

But maybe things had at last settled down in town, now that a new vein was being explored. Maybe that's why Pa could spend a quiet evening at home rather than break up another fight between miners gone crazy from fear and worry.

Jem took a swallow of milk and blurted, "I reckon I can start delivering frog legs to the café again, right, Pa?"

Pa looked surprised at Jem's question. "Why would you think that?" He popped a forkful of fluffy dumpling in his mouth and chewed.

"Well, you're home tonight. It must mean the miners know the Midas will reopen soon, and they're calming down. No riots. No fights. Right?" Jem searched Pa's face for a satisfying answer.

"Hardly. I took a chance and left a temporary deputy in charge—No-luck Casey." Pa reached for his coffee cup. "He's pretty green at the job, but he's happy to earn fifty cents a day. It's more than he finds in that played-out claim of his."

Jem's heart sank. "But Chad told me they found a new vein. It's a deep one that might stretch for—"

"Did he tell you that this new, deep vein needs an air shaft?" Pa broke in. "And did he tell you *where* this new air shaft will be located?" His eyes flashed.

Jem lost his appetite at the memory. "The Belle diggings."

"That's right." Pa pushed his plate back. It looked like he'd lost his appetite as well. And no wonder. Wu Shen's kinfolk stood in the way of reopening the Midas mine. "Mr. Sterling wants his old mine back."

"Can he do that?" Jem asked. He'd told Chad that Wu Shen's folks owned the claim, but maybe Jem was wrong. Grown-ups could do a lot of things—especially *important* grown-ups. And Mr. Sterling was the most important grown-up in Goldtown.

"No, he can't," Pa said. "Scavenger laws are binding, and the Wu claim is on the town books. I checked."

Jem let out a quiet breath of relief, but it was short-lived. If Mr. Sterling could not go through his old mine for an air shaft, what would happen to the Midas? Or the town?

Pa was still talking, so Jem pricked up his ears and listened. Nathan and Ellie, who had been hungrily stuffing chicken and dumplings into their mouths, paused in their eating to listen too. Even Aunt Rose looked interested.

"Trouble is, everybody in town knows the Belle used to belong to Sterling," Pa continued. "I remember when he and his partners worked those diggings. The easy gold played out after a couple of years. His partners moved on, and Sterling abandoned the Belle. He eventually went on to survey and open the Midas."

Pa leaned back in his chair and frowned. "He didn't care when the Chinese moved in and began to work those old diggings. He laughed and said it was a good joke on them. 'The gold's gone, but it will keep the Chinamen out of our hair,' he told me. Well, the joke's on Sterling because Wu's kinfolk managed to scrape up what little gold was left. The Chinese are a patient people. They're not getting rich, but they're getting by."

"They sure do work hard," Jem agreed when Pa stopped

for breath. "Wu Shen's always hauling cartloads of laundry around town or carrying supplies up to the diggings. I don't understand why the town bullies pick on him so much."

Pa slammed his chair forward and sat up straight. "They're not just picking on Wu Shen, Jem. Yesterday, I broke up a group of men who were bullying some Chinese miners—telling them to get off the claim or they'd drive them off. Come to find out, those rowdies were acting under Mr. Sterling's orders." Pa curled his fist and slammed it down on the table.

Jem, Ellie, and Nathan jumped. Pa hardly ever let his anger sneak out.

"I'm sorry," Pa apologized. He took a deep breath. "Air shaft or no air shaft, Mr. Sterling is not above the law. If the Chinese want to stay and work their mine, then it's my job to make sure they can."

Jem forced down his last bite of dumpling. It suddenly tasted like sawdust. "Mr. Sterling's not going to like you going against him."

Pa shook his head. "No sirree, he sure isn't. In fact, we've already had words." Pa didn't say what those words were, and Jem didn't ask. But knowing Will's father, Jem could take a good guess that Mr. Sterling's words were loud, mean-mouthed, and bossy.

I wish Pa wasn't the sheriff. The thought came before Jem could squash it. A few weeks ago, he'd finally stopped fretting over Pa being sheriff. Seeing Pa's skill with a gun had gone a long way in easing Jem's fears that some crazy, drunken outlaw would go after the new sheriff.

But now that old worry popped right back into Jem's head. Nearly a hundred miners were on the loose—angry and fearful over losing their jobs. Pa couldn't control them all, especially if he was the only one who stood between the Chinese scavengers and the angry miners.

Especially if Mr. Sterling stood against him.

⚔ CHAPTER 11 ⚔

Scavenger Diggings

A banging on the door the next morning roused Jem from picking at his bowl of oatmeal. He didn't like the sticky, hot mush even on a good day, which this one wasn't. He hadn't slept well last night.

The early morning callers gave him an excuse to push his breakfast away. "I'll get it." He sprang from his seat before anyone else at the table blinked.

Jem jerked the door open then winced. His left arm still burned from yesterday's branding mishap. "Come in," he told the two visitors standing on the threshold. "We're having breakfast. You're welcome to join us. That is, if you like oatmeal." He made a face.

"No, thank you," Mr. Carter said. "We've eaten. Although"— he looked at Chad—"you might still be hungry, Son. What do you say? Care for a bowl of mush?"

"It's Aunt Rose's specialty," Jem added with a smirk.

Chad stumbled around for words. "Uh . . . no. No thanks. I'm good." The look on his face showed that he hated oatmeal as much as Jem did.

Laughing, Mr. Carter clapped Chad on the back and ushered him into the small front room. "I wouldn't say no to a cup of coffee," he said.

Pa joined the visitors and reached out to shake the rancher's hand. "Coffee's hot. Come on back to the kitchen and pull up a chair."

By the time Jem returned to the table, his oatmeal was cold and beyond eating. Aunt Rose bustled around to show the guests their seats and pour a cup of coffee for Mr. Carter. Jem used her distraction to scrape the rest of his oatmeal into the chicken bucket. The Coulters' two dozen hens and Mordecai the rooster would soon enjoy the offering.

Jem returned to his seat and felt his cousin's gaze boring into him. Then Nathan slipped from the table and tried the same trick.

"Nathan Frederick," Aunt Rose scolded, returning to her place at the table. "You sit right back down and finish that mush. The very idea! Wasting good food on chickens."

"But, Mother!" Nathan protested. He gave Jem a you-lucky-dog look. Then he slumped in his chair and choked down the rest of his breakfast.

Jem knew better than to gloat. Aunt Rose had eyes not only in the back of her head, but on each side too. As often as she caught Jem and Ellie in mischief, she clearly knew her own son much better. He never got away with anything. Jem shrugged at his cousin to show his sympathy.

"What can I do for you, Mr. Carter?" Pa asked when his guests had settled themselves around the crowded table. "It's mighty early in the day to be calling on folks."

"First off, you can call me James," the rancher replied, sipping his coffee. "Fine coffee, ma'am," he told Aunt Rose, who beamed. Then he returned his attention to Pa, and his tone became serious. "How well do you know the Chinese miners up at the Belle diggings?"

Jem froze. He'd been about to ask if Chad wanted to go outside and give him a hand chopping firewood for this week's deliveries. However, at the mention of the Belle diggings, Jem quickly changed his mind. He fiddled with his cold toast and took to heart his aunt's favorite mealtime saying: "Children should not speak unless spoken to."

Pa never paid any mind to his older sister's attempts to enforce this bit of table etiquette. He liked to hear his children share their day. But right now, Jem knew that the less he talked, the more he'd learn.

Pa shrugged. "Casual acquaintance, I reckon. The Chinese don't mix in much, but there's never been any trouble between us. I know most of them by name, if that's what you're asking." He paused. "Why?"

Mr. Carter scratched his chin, took another sip of coffee, and said, "Sterling and I can't seem to agree about what's to be done with the Belle diggings. He's worked himself up into quite a tizzy over it. He wants those scavengers out, and he wants them out quick. I do agree that the only way to save the Midas is to somehow recover the Belle."

A sudden chill fell over the room, even though the rising sun streamed through the kitchen window. Jem's heart pounded against his ribcage. He exchanged a look with Chad, who stared back, unblinking. *Chad probably wishes he was home branding calves rather than caught up in this mining mess.*

Pa let out a long, slow breath. "You were there when Sterling and I had words the other day. You know where I stand." He stood up. "I've got work to do before I head for town, and the day's a'wastin'. So, if you'll excuse me?"

Mr. Carter rose too. "You misunderstand me, Sheriff. I'm not asking you to go along with Sterling's plan to drive out the scavengers. Far from it. I realize he has no claim to the Belle." He paused. "But I may have a solution."

Pa slowly returned to his seat. "I'm listening."

Jem was listening too—with both ears.

"I believe the easiest way to solve this problem is to simply buy the mine."

Jem's eyes opened wide. A gasp nearly escaped, but he held it back. Respect for Chad's father rose a couple of notches. *What a jim-dandy idea!*

Pa didn't look as if *he* thought it was such a great idea. He wrinkled his brow, drummed his fingers against the table, and grunted. "You won't get far with that idea. Ernest Sterling is not much for buying what he thinks already belongs to him."

Mr. Carter chuckled. "You certainly know your townspeople, Sheriff. Those were practically his exact words. But no matter. I intend to buy the mine myself. I will make the Chinese a fair offer—a generous offer."

Respect for Chad's father rose even higher. Pretty soon, Mr. Carter would be near the top of Jem's list of favorite people, right up there beside Pa and Strike-it-rich Sam. This rich rancher could easily run home to his fancy spread down south and leave Goldtown to worry about its future. He didn't need the wealth from any gold mines. Why would he care enough to buy those worthless diggings just so the Midas could have its air shaft?

Pa's eyes had widened during Mr. Carter's words, but before he could respond, the rancher went on. "Could you go out to the diggings with me, Sheriff, when I make my offer? I'm a stranger, but the Chinese miners know you. They might listen if you ask them to. It's worth a try. The air shaft is vital, and this seems the only way to get it."

"I'll go," Pa said. "I'm just as anxious as Sterling to save the mine and the town." He rose and reached for his hat. "By the way, you can call me Matt."

It took a bit of coaxing, but Jem managed to wrangle his way into going along to the Belle diggings. He felt a little sorry when he mounted Copper and pulled up beside Chad behind the men. A quick glance over his shoulder showed Ellie hanging on the porch railing, giving Jem a fierce glare. Nathan's nose pushed up against the screen door. He looked just as annoyed as Ellie.

"I'm not dragging all of you along," Pa had said when three voices clamored to be included. "This is not a Sunday-school picnic, but serious matters. Jem's the oldest and nearly grown, so he can go." He'd given his son a serious look. "Maybe after today, you'll understand why I'd rather starve on our ranch than work in a hard-rock mine."

"I reckon Pa wants me to 'widen my horizons,'" Jem joked with Chad as they trailed behind their fathers, "just like you."

Chad rolled his eyes and muttered something about wishing he were branding the Coulters' calves right about now. Or panning for gold. ". . . or riding a decent horse," he finished with a grunt. "Anything but plodding along on this jughead."

Next to Copper, Chad's mount did look like a worn-out, scruffy nag. Even Strike's donkey, Canary, looked nicer. "I'm surprised the Sterlings keep such a flea-bitten horse in their stables," Jem said.

Chad let out a loud sigh. "They don't. This is my punishment for taking off with Prince Charming yesterday. Father went to the livery in town and picked out the sorriest-looking hay-burner there. Good thing our ranch hands back home can't see me." His cheeks turned red. "They'd laugh their heads off."

Jem nearly burst trying to keep his own laughter inside. He clapped a hand over his mouth and nudged Copper into a trot so Chad couldn't see his face. Teasing words like "Wanna race?" popped into his head, but he pushed them back. No sense ruining a perfectly good friendship with a mean mouth.

Besides, he didn't know Chad very well. The boy might

have a temper and light into him. Seeing his size, Jem knew he didn't stand a chance against Chad in a fight.

When they reached the diggings, thoughts of teasing Chad or caring about what kind of horse he rode flew from Jem's mind. One look at the black, gaping hole of the old Belle mine sent eager shivers racing up and down Jem's spine.

A ribbon of water trickled through a narrow, rocky 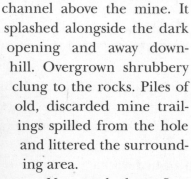 channel above the mine. It splashed alongside the dark opening and away down-hill. Overgrown shrubbery clung to the rocks. Piles of old, discarded mine trail-ings spilled from the hole and littered the surround-ing area.

Now and then, Jem helped Wu Shen cart sup-plies up the steep, winding road to the Belle diggings. Shen's family always traded for his help with crispy rice cakes, which Jem munched on his way back down. But he had never been inside.

"I reckon you've been in lots of mines," Chad said. He sounded envious.

Jem pulled Copper to a standstill. "Nope. Wu Shen never invited me. I've never been in the Midas, either."

"Really?"

Jem nodded. "Ellie and I've crawled around inside doz-ens of small coyote holes though."

Chad looked disgusted. "*Coyote* holes? Why would you—"

"Not *real* coyote holes," Jem said, laughing. "Mining holes. They're everywhere in the gold fields. Prospectors call 'em coyote holes. Some are pretty deep. But they're not very interesting. Most are just empty holes. No gold."

Chad grinned. "So this is the first time inside a real mine for both of us."

"Yep."

Pa and Mr. Carter had brought lanterns along. They dismounted, lit the kerosene lamps, and motioned the boys to follow.

Jem's heart thumped in a mixture of dread and delight. He stepped through the black opening and was instantly transported into an eerie, silent world. Silent, except for the constant drip of groundwater from overhead and the faint *tap, tap, tap* of several picks and hammers from deep inside.

Jem was glad to discover he could stand up straight and walk normally. So could Pa and Mr. Carter, who were tall. Jem had envisioned the Belle diggings as nothing more than an oversized coyote hole—cramped and suffocating. This mine seemed roomy.

"I didn't think it would be this big," he said.

"Compared to the Midas," Pa said, "this is a shallow hole in the ground." He lifted his lantern and tapped the rocky ceiling. "Only rock holds this mine up, and there's not much of it between here and the surface. The Midas, on the other hand, is shored up with solid wood beams. It also has numerous side tunnels, and tracks for the ore carts. It's a big operation." He paused. "It *was*, anyway."

"And it will be again," Chad's father added firmly, "God willing."

Jem stuck close to his father's heels—and the light—as they followed a set of rusting tracks deeper into the mine. To Jem's surprise, the ground did not slant down much. It cut into the hill with hardly any turns.

Pa stopped and held his lantern to the side. A gaping blackness lay two feet away. "Watch for holes. Prospectors went crazy in here. They dug every which way, into the walls and even in the floor. The holes aren't deep, but you could break a leg if you stepped in one."

"They cut this mine by hand?" Jem gulped. "That would take years!"

"Sterling used blasting powder off and on," Pa answered, "but that caused more problems than it solved. The Chinese are chipping away by hand."

The tapping sounded louder now, and Jem could see a far-off glow from many lanterns. He shivered. It was cold and clammy underground. Drop by drop, the seeping water splashed on his head.

"Ugh!" Chad swiped water from his face and looked at Jem. "Glad I'm not a miner."

The tapping and clanging suddenly stopped. Jem heard whispers, scraping, and the sound of shuffling feet. A Chinese man approached, holding his lantern high. He was dressed in a dirty, ragged tunic and loose-fitting pants. His free hand clutched a pickax.

"What do you want here?" he demanded in good English. The lantern light bounced off the rocks, revealing a trembling hand.

Behind him, five or six others appeared, armed with pickaxes, shovels, and wary scowls. Jem caught his breath. It was clearly not the first time these miners had greeted unwelcome visitors to their claim. Then he remembered what Pa had said at supper last night. Mr. Sterling was urging the men in town to force the scavengers from their mine. No wonder they looked worried.

Pa stepped forward. Jem stayed back. "It's Sheriff Coulter, Wu Hao."

86

"Have you come with threats from Sterling, Sheriff?" Wu Hao growled.

"No," Pa assured him. "Look"—he swept his hand to take in Jem and Chad—"I brought my son and another boy. It's a friendly visit. Mr. Carter would like to talk to you about your mine. Then we'll leave." He spread his hands out. "Will you put down your picks and listen?"

Wu Hao searched the sheriff's face then set down his pickax and seemed to relax. His comrades did not. The Chinese miner spoke to the men behind him. They shuffled, talked in short, excited bursts, then backed off.

Wu Hao turned to Pa. "We will listen. But only because we respect you, Sheriff. Whatever this man has to say, it will not change our minds. We pay our tax. The mine is ours."

"I understand," Pa said.

"Come." Wu Hao lifted his lantern and led them to the end of the tunnel. Half a dozen Chinese surrounded them in watchful silence, still gripping their mining tools. Their broad, golden faces seemed carved from stone. Long black pigtails hung down their backs. A rusting ore cart took up most of this section of the mine. It was half filled with ore hacked from the sides and roof of the tunnel. From overhead, small rocks crumbled and fell in a pebbly shower.

What a miserable way to make a living, Jem thought, ducking out of the way.

Someone must have been working on the mine's ceiling just before the visitors came calling. Without warning, more rocks loosened and fell. Jem flattened himself against the tunnel wall and held his breath.

Pa shouted a warning and lunged at Wu Hao just as a section of the tunnel's ceiling came crashing down.

ᢞ CHAPTER 12 ᢟ

Taking Sides

Jem flung his arms over his head, squeezed his eyes shut, and waited for the rocks and dust to settle. There was nothing he could do to help. Staying out of harm's way seemed the best choice. Something soft and squishy slammed against Jem, knocking him to the ground. When he opened his eyes, Chad lay half-sprawled on top of him.

Jem shoved the heavier boy aside and sat up. His eyes watered from the fine dust that hung thick in the air. He sneezed.

Chad groaned and rubbed his arm. "That was close. A big rock just missed me."

Pa hurried over. "You boys all right?" He slapped dust and debris from his arms and shoulders and let out a relieved breath. "One of the daily hazards of mining these old claims," he explained. "You never know when the section you're working on will take a notion to let loose and come down on top of you."

Jem glanced down at the quartz ore scattered at his feet. *Give me a gold pan and a creek any day.* One second the rocks were part of the mine's ceiling. A second later they were part of the floor. *If Pa hadn't shoved Wu Hao out of the way, he'd be . . .* Jem shuddered.

Wu Hao shook the dirt from his tunic and stepped forward. He nodded toward the rubble. "Thank you, Sheriff, for your quick hands and feet. We did not expect the rock to break loose so suddenly. Many days we have worked on it." He looked pleased. The fact that he'd almost found himself under the debris didn't seem to faze him. "We have much work. You go now."

The Chinese descended on the mound of ore like a flock of vultures on a steer's carcass. They ignored their unwelcome guests and hurried to examine the rocks and pile them into the cart. Their voices rose in eagerness.

"What about—" Jem started to say.

Pa cut him off him with a frown and joined the busy miners. "You agreed to listen to my friend. It won't take long."

An impatient look crossed Wu Hao's face, but he straightened and gave Pa a curt nod. "Very well. Since you, Sheriff, think it best, we will listen. But say it quickly so we can return to our work." The others paused and waited.

Mr. Carter stepped forward. "Thank you. I'll make this short and simple. I would like to buy your mine."

The men reacted with soft gasps and quick intakes of breath. They had clearly not expected such an offer. The startled look in Wu Hao's eyes faded, and he wrinkled his brow. "You would buy what you tried to take?"

"I had no part in that ugly business, Wu Hao," Chad's father said. "I've come to offer you a fair and honest price. Whatever you think your mine is worth."

The Chinese miner frowned then motioned to his companions. They moved off and began speaking together in their own language. Jem listened as their singsong voices rose and fell. *Please say yes!* he pleaded silently.

Finally, Wu Hao broke away from the others and stood before Pa and Mr. Carter. He shook his head. "Sterling deals with blows. You come with words. Neither will drive us out. The mine is not for sale."

Jem's shoulders slumped. Didn't they care what happened to Goldtown?

Mr. Carter didn't appear ready to take no for an answer. He squared his shoulders and pressed harder. "Perhaps you don't understand how important this is. To reopen the Midas, the tunnels must go deep—far deeper than ever before. The men can't breathe down there without ventilation. An air shaft will go straight up, and it needs to go through this mine. Without it, the Midas will close. The miners will have no way to earn a living."

Wu Hao didn't blink. "We also need the mine to make a living." He picked up a fist-sized rock from the pile of rubble. "Do you see these specks? It is gold. Not a lot, but enough to live."

"I will pay you well," Mr. Carter urged. He took the ore from Wu Hao, examined it closely, and handed it back. "More than enough to make up for any gold you might find now or in the future. You can buy another business."

"Where?"

"Here, or anywhere you like."

Wu Hao gave a short, bitter laugh. "And . . . if somebody decide they want *that* business, will we be asked to sell it also?" He let the rock fall from his hand. "Six years ago they drive us from our claim in Drytown. We come here, hoping to put down roots and make a place for ourselves." He shook his head. "We will not pull up roots again."

Jem knew all about roots being pulled up. For years, each school term began with empty seats, seats that once held Jem's and Ellie's friends. When prospectors moved on to fresh diggings, they dragged their families with them. The seats were soon filled with new faces from other gold camps.

Thankfully, the opening of the Midas mine had changed

all that. But now, if Goldtown died, *everyone's* roots would be yanked up. "It's for the good of everybody in town," Jem burst out. Then he clamped his jaw shut. Pa was giving him his you-keep-quiet look.

Wu Hao turned to Jem. "We are not treated like everybody in town."

Jem flushed at the memory of last week. The Chinese miner was right. Jem's wagonload of firewood had interrupted the town bullies from ganging up on his friend Wu Shen. *I sure put my foot in my mouth this time!*

Pa clearly agreed. "Jeremiah, why don't you and Chad go out for some fresh air? Mr. Carter and I will be along in a minute."

When Jem started to protest, Pa shook his head and passed him the lantern. Chad plucked Jem's sleeve, and together the two boys hurried back the way they'd come. "And mind you keep a lookout for holes," Pa's voice echoed after them.

Jem strained to hear the tail end of the adults' conversation.

"And you, Sheriff?" Wu Hao asked. "Do you agree? Must we give up our mine?"

"I won't take sides," came Pa's faint reply. "It's your choice, and the law is on your side. But the offer to buy your mine is an honest one."

Jem didn't catch Wu Hao's reply. He didn't have to. Mr. Carter could talk from now until sundown, and it wouldn't make a difference. The Chinese scavengers appeared stuck tight as ticks to their diggings.

Chad gave a long, low whistle when he and Jem broke out into the bright, morning sunshine. "That miner paid Father no more mind than if he were a chattering chipmunk," he said. "Now there's going to be *real* trouble."

Jem wished Wu Hao had agreed to sell the mine, but he

hadn't. The mine owners would just have to think of something else. "What trouble?" he shot at Chad. "The law is on Wu Hao's side. There's nothing Mr. Sterling can do about that."

Chad snorted. "You're talking like your greenhorn, city cousin now. Since when does spouting off the law make everybody follow it?"

Jem bristled.

"Mr. Sterling's the biggest frog in the puddle around here," Chad said, wagging his head. "He can do plenty. The law may be on the scavengers' side, but your father is the law. He said he wouldn't take sides, but"—Chad glanced back at the mine opening—"he just did."

Pa didn't say much when he and Mr. Carter came out of the mine. He mounted up and headed just where Jem figured he'd go—straight to the Sterling mansion. Jem didn't know what he should do. Follow along? Go back to the ranch? Pa hadn't sent him home, so maybe he'd see how it played out. Pa had a way with words. Folks usually listened when he spoke.

"It won't be fun for the sheriff to break bad news to an important person like Mr. Sterling," Chad whispered when the grown-ups were well ahead of the boys.

Jem didn't answer. He hoped Chad was wrong. Mr. Sterling knew the law. He and Chad's pa could come up with another idea for the air shaft. Surely, Mr. Sterling wouldn't act like a low-down claim jumper and try to steal Wu Hao's mine. He *couldn't*. If he did, Pa would have to arrest him like any other lawbreaker.

Jem swallowed. What a terrible idea!

"Aren't you coming?" Chad yelled.

Jem jerked from his dismal thoughts and focused on the

riders in front of him. It wasn't a long way from the old Belle diggings to the Sterling place, but he'd fallen behind. He slammed his heels into Copper's sides. "Giddup!"

Copper snorted and shot ahead. Jem grimaced when he rode past the deserted stamp mill. It stood as eerily silent as the week before, when Jem had gotten a taste of the miners' feelings about losing their livelihoods. At the time, their anger had boiled over onto the mine superintendent and Mr. Sterling. Now, it had shifted. Only a handful of Chinese scavengers stood between the miners and their jobs.

Jem caught up just as they reached the Sterling mansion. The sun reflected off Pa's silver star when he dismounted. The shiny badge reminded Jem how dangerous a sheriff's job could get. The old, familiar fear for Pa's safety began to creep into Jem's thoughts. Before it could freeze his mind, Jem squeezed his eyes shut and prayed.

God, I thought worrying was behind me, what with Pa being a crack shot an' all. Now, all of a sudden, I'm scared again. What if Pa has to stand against the whole town, on account of a few Chinese scavengers? Please don't let that happen. Give Pa the right words to say to Mr. Sterling.

Jem gulped and finished his prayer in a hurry. *And, God? Make me brave enough to stand with Pa, 'cause right now I'm not sure where I stand. I think I'd just as soon Wu Shen and his family left the mine . . . any way they can.*

There. He'd said it. Maybe not out loud, but he'd said it to God. He felt disloyal not only to his friend Wu Shen—and his family's right to work their claim—but to Pa as well.

Trouble was, Jem didn't know *whose* side he was on. Not anymore.

CHAPTER 13

From Bad to Worse

From the first knock, Jem knew things would go badly. A grim-faced Mr. Sterling opened the door and stepped out on the wide veranda. It looked like he'd been awaiting their arrival and had shooed the housekeeper away to greet his guests alone. He did not invite them inside. Instead, he closed the door behind him, crossed his arms over his broad chest, and narrowed his eyes.

"Well?"

"I did my best, Ernest," Mr. Carter said with a shrug, "but apparently their mine is not for sale."

"*Their* mine!" Mr. Sterling scoffed. "I told you it was a waste of time, James. All those scavengers understand is force. Well, don't worry. They'll get out." He uncrossed his arms and pointed a meaty finger in the sheriff's direction. "I want you to evict those claim jumpers, Sheriff."

Pa let out a breath. "I can't do that, and you know it. It's their claim."

"Scavenger claims don't count in my book."

Pa's expression turned hard. "They count in the town's book, and that's all I'm interested in."

Mr. Sterling stepped across the porch until he and the

sheriff stood nose to nose. "I dug that tunnel!" he shouted in Pa's face. "There wouldn't be any mine if I hadn't opened it up all those years ago. And there won't be any town if the Midas shuts down. No. More. Goldtown." He punctuated each word with a jab to Pa's chest. "Do you understand?"

Jem wanted to plug his ears and hightail it home. Or punch Mr. Sterling. How could Pa stand there and let Mr. Sterling bully him?

Pa didn't flinch. He didn't back down. He didn't yell. "Of course I understand," he said. "I want that air shaft as much as you and James do. But you'll have to find another way. You can't take Wu Hao's claim."

Mr. Sterling deflated like a leaky balloon. "You would let this town die for a handful of scavengers? Whose side are you on, Sheriff Coulter?"

It took Pa no time to answer. "When it's the miners destroying your property, I'm on your side, Ernest. When it's you trying to jump somebody's legal claim, I'm on theirs."

Mr. Sterling's face turned red. His jabbing finger returned to Pa's chest. "Let me tell you something, Sheriff. James Carter and I do not intend to simply throw up our hands and—"

"Sorry, Ernest," Mr. Carter broke in. "I can't be a part of this. I'm with the sheriff. Forcing those scavengers out is wrong . . . and illegal."

Mr. Sterling whirled on his houseguest. "Are you crazy, James? Do you know what this means?" He didn't wait for an answer but took a step back and grunted, "I'll deal with this myself. No need for you to get your fingers dirty."

He turned to Pa. "The circuit judge is due in town any day. If you haven't the gumption to throw those scavengers out, we'll see what Judge Reece has to say. In the meantime, *Sheriff*"—his eyes glinted dangerously—"I suggest you keep to your ranch and out of town."

Pa stood his ground. "I hope that's not a threat, Ernest. If it is, and you stir up more trouble in town, I'll be right there—along with my deputies—to see that your rowdy miners behave themselves."

Mr. Sterling snorted. "I doubt you'll be able to hire any deputies. They know which side their bread is buttered on."

Jem's stomach churned listening to Mr. Sterling's mean-mouthed threats. The mine owner's tongue shot hot little word darts, poking Pa, trying to make him back down and give in. Pity for Will suddenly pricked at the back of Jem's mind. If Mr. Sterling talked to his children half as mean as he was bossing Pa, then no wonder Will acted like he did.

Help me not to fly into Will the next time he acts up or shows off, Jem prayed. *If Pa can stand there and take it, so can I . . . well . . . maybe.*

Watching Pa stand up to Mr. Sterling gave Jem an idea. He still didn't know which side he was on—*whichever side keeps Pa safe*, he told himself—but there was something he could do to stand up to Mr. Sterling's mean and bossy ways. Besides, he was sick of listening to him.

"Pa," Jem broke in. He was too upset to worry about his bad manners. "I've got something I have to do. I'll see you back at the ranch, if that's all right."

Pa raised his eyebrows but said nothing. He nodded and turned back to Mr. Sterling, who seemed not to have noticed Jem's rude interruption. The mine owner was on another rant. Chad made a move toward Jem, but Jem shook his head. This was something he had to do himself. Chad slumped. Clearly, he wanted a reason to escape the charged air. It seemed to crackle around the three men.

Jem clomped down the porch steps and around to the kitchen entrance. Saturday was firewood delivery day. He had to talk to Cook before then. He rapped on the door and waited. Then he waited some more. Another rap, harder this time. It was almost noon. Surely, the Sterling's cook was inside preparing the meal. A curtain hung across the glass pane in the door. It was no use trying to peer inside to see what was going on.

Jem was lifting his fist to bang on the windowpane when the door opened. Will stood in the doorway, munching on the biggest sugar cookie Jem had ever seen. "What do *you* want?" Will demanded between mouthfuls.

None of your business nearly flew from Jem's mouth, but he bit the words back. "Is your cook around?" he asked.

Will popped the rest of the cookie in his mouth and swiped a careless sleeve across his face. It didn't help much. Cookie crumbs stuck to his cheeks like pale freckles. "She's busy."

Jem waited, but Will did not offer to fetch the cook. He didn't invite Jem inside. He just stood there, studying him.

"May I talk to her?" Jem finally asked. He wanted to shove his way inside. Will was baiting him, trying to make him lose his temper. It nearly choked him, but Jem added, "Please?"

Will smirked and flung the door open all the way. "I suppose. Come on in."

He left Jem standing in the kitchen. The black cook stove radiated a stifling heat. Pots and pans bubbled; a tea kettle whistled. The odor of roast beef and boiling potatoes made Jem's stomach rumble. *This meal is not for you,* he told his belly.

Will returned a minute later with Cook. He snatched another cookie from a cooling rack and said, "Make it fast, Jem. Cook's busy."

Cook rounded on Will. Her gray eyes snapped. "I'll have none of your lip in my kitchen, Master William, or the missus'll hear about you snackin' between meals."

Will gulped and nodded.

Jem hid a grin. It was clear who ruled the Sterlings' kitchen.

Cook turned to Jem with a smile. "What can I be doin' for you today, Jem? It's not Saturday. Are you delivering wood early?"

"No, ma'am. I . . ." Jem paused to see if Will would leave the room and give them some privacy. He didn't. The sneaky weasel settled himself on top of a stool, all ears. *I should have known. Well, no matter.* "I came to tell you that I won't be delivering your firewood anymore."

Cook threw up her hands. "Merciful heavens! Why not?"

Will stopped chewing. His brown eyes bugged out. Jem knew why. Every boy in town clamored for the Sterlings' firewood business. Jem had offers to swap for it every few months.

"Well . . ." Jem squirmed. Then he took a deep breath and let his words tumble out. He didn't care if Will heard them. "My pa's having a rough time right now. He's standing up against Mr. Sterling, even though he doesn't want to see the mine fail and Goldtown die. But he's got no choice, not like the rest of the town. He's the sheriff and has to uphold the law." Jem swallowed. "Even for scavengers."

Will's mouth dropped open.

Jem squared his shoulders. "I reckon I can take a stand too and drop Mr. Sterling from my route. I want to show him that even though I'm not sure if I'm on the scavengers' side, I *am* on Pa's side." His shoulders slumped. "I know Cole Thompson wants this route. He's reliable. I'll let him know he can have it."

Cook didn't answer for a moment. Instead, she pressed her lips together and blinked. Then she took a corner of her apron and wiped her eyes. "I'm sorry to lose you, Jem," she finally said. "But goodness! Wouldn't your mama be proud if she could see you now." She thrust a warm sugar cookie into Jem's hand. "Here. You go along now and don't be worrin' 'bout your pa. The good Lord'll take care of all this, you'll see."

"Yes, ma'am," Jem mumbled. "Thank you, ma'am." He jammed the sugary treat into his mouth and left in a hurry, anxious to get away before Will could tease him. Jem could hear him now: *I knew you were a fool, Jem, but to give up the best customer in all of Goldtown makes you dumber than dumb.*

Without the Sterlings, Jem's firewood business would take a permanent nosedive. He'd already lost the Big Strike, when Pa pulled the plug on delivering sawdust to a saloon. Now he was down to two firewood customers and a scant handful of folks who wanted frog legs. With summer in full swing, his frog-leg business would soon dry up too.

"I'm gonna be broke," Jem mourned as he mounted Copper and urged him toward home. Not even the extra free time to pan for gold cheered him. By late summer, Cripple Creek would be dried up to a mere trickle, making it extra hard to wash gold.

Alone with his thoughts, Jem plodded down the winding road from Belle Hill to town. He didn't turn around when he heard the sound of hoofbeats clattering behind him. *It's probably Chad, wanting to pan more gold.* Jem didn't feel like going to the creek. Besides, he had about a million chores waiting for him at home.

"Hey, Jem!" Will's nasal voice pierced the air.

Roasted rattlesnakes! Why can't Will leave me alone? He readied his heels above Copper's flank. One swift kick and Prince Charming would be left in the dust. Literally. But the look on Will's face when he pulled up beside Copper made Jem tuck in his feet and pause. "What do you want?"

"Nothin'," Will replied. "I'm headed for town. Thought I'd ride along with you."

"Why?" Jem didn't know what to make of Will's sudden show of friendliness.

Will shrugged. "No reason, I guess." Then he sighed. "All right. There's a reason. Father's been in a ranting, yelling, stomping rage all week. I had to get outta there." He eyed Jem. "He's mad as all get out at your pa, and now . . ." His voice trailed off.

"Yeah?" Jem urged. "Now *what*?"

"The Carters are moving to the hotel in town. They must not like my father's mood any better than I do."

"If they're smart, they'll go back to their ranch," Jem muttered.

Will cracked a smile. "Yeah."

Jem rounded the corner to Main Street and shrugged. "See ya, Will." It was the polite thing to say, even though he hoped he didn't see Will Sterling or his father for a long, long time. Will waved and went his own way. A couple more blocks and Jem would be rid of the town and back on the ranch. He planned to stay there until all this mine business blew over. Safer that way.

A sudden squeal of pain and terror pulled Jem away from his plans. A group of boys half a block away surrounded Wu Shen. They were bullying him. Again. Jem's anger burned red hot. He might not agree with the Chinese miners' decision to hold on to their mine, but he would not let anyone pick on his friend.

"Leave him alone!" he shouted, urging Copper forward.

The boys ignored Jem and continued to attack Shen. Dutch Warner overturned Shen's two-wheeled pushcart. One wheel came loose, and his load of laundry went flying. Tom Lange clutched a fistful of Shen's long pigtail. Even Jem's friend Cole was taking part. He had Shen by one arm, holding him tight, while two others threw swift punches at their helpless victim.

Furious, Jem plowed Copper into the middle of the group. Now they would listen! A cry of surprise and rage mixed with Copper's whinny and Shen's screeching. Cole and another boy fled, one cradling his arm and limping.

"I hope Copper stepped on your foot!" Jem yelled after him. He looked around. Tom and Dutch had dodged the horse and were hitting and pulling at Shen. Freddy Stone held him tight. Jem yanked on Copper's reins. The horse shied to the left and rammed into Tom.

Tom reached out and snagged Jem's ankle, keeping his balance. Then he curled his other hand around Jem's leg and yanked. Other eager hands grasped Jem's britches and shirt. With a triumphant shout, the boys pulled Jem off his horse and into the fray.

❧ CHAPTER 14 ❧

Fight!

Jem came up swinging. He knew if he stayed on the ground, he was done for. Tom and the others would pile on top of him, and that would be the end of it. A sudden punch to his still-tender "brand" sent searing pain up Jem's arm, making him reel backward with a gasp. He curled his fist and drove it straight for Tom's face.

Jem might as well have tried to hit a fly in mid-air. Tom ducked the blow, grasped Jem's shoulders, and spun him around. Freddy's fist plunged into Jem's stomach. He collapsed in a crumpled heap.

"Stay outta this, Jem." Tom swiped a hank of dirty brown hair from his face and glowered. "I got no reason to fight you. "

Jem sucked in air to steady his shaking arms and legs then staggered to his feet. He faced the three bullies, clenching his fists. For ten whole seconds, nobody moved a muscle or blinked an eye. "Leave Shen alone," Jem finally said between clenched teeth.

Tom curled his lip. "You've got one chance, Jem. Walk away. *Now.*"

Jem's hammering heart skipped a beat. What was Tom

up to? Once the older boy got riled, he never backed down. Why would he give Jem a chance to escape? *Run and find Pa,* Jem's good sense told him. His throbbing arm and belly screamed the same command.

One look at Wu Shen sent all good sense flying from Jem's head. *I don't have time to find Pa.* Blood smeared the Chinese boy's nose and mouth. Dutch held him fast with one hand. His other hand clutched a pocketknife. Jem caught his breath.

Dutch laughed. "I'm just gonna give the China boy a haircut. A little message to the scavengers to get out before somethin' worse happens." He yanked hard on Shen's pigtail. The boy winced.

"What you do right now, Jem," Tom said, "will show if you're on the town's side or on the side of dirty, yellow scavengers." He paused and spat. "We *know* where the sheriff stands. But it ain't your fault your pa's a—"

"Shut up!" A hot flush soared through Jem at Tom's words. How dare he insult Pa! The flush raced down his arm and made his hand curl up almost on its own. He raised his fist and smashed it head-on into Dutch's sneering face. Blood spurted from his nose. *Bull's eye!*

"Run, Shen!" Jem shouted.

Dutch howled and dropped his knife. But he didn't let go of Shen. The Chinese boy reached down and bit his captor's hand then wrenched free. He took two steps toward freedom before Freddy yanked him back into Dutch's grip.

Jem was rubbing his sore knuckles when Tom came for him—shoulders heaving and roaring like a bull. Down the two boys went, rolling and scuffling in the dusty street. "Reckon we'll give the sheriff a message about which side *he* should choose," Tom hissed in Jem's ear.

Jem was too busy focusing on staying in one piece to answer. One-on-one, Jem and Tom were equally matched, and Jem was angry enough to emerge the victor. But two to one? Or three to one? *If only Shen would lend a hand and defend himself, maybe we'd have a chance,* Jem thought as he warded off another blow.

Even if he'd wanted to help, Shen's slight build was no match for the taller, heavier boys. He was clawing and biting the best he could, but Dutch ignored his own bleeding nose and gripped Shen's pigtail like a leash on a dog. He landed his punches with little effort.

When Freddy joined Tom, Jem knew he would lose this fight. His head felt like it might explode any second. A hard smack had reopened the gash from last week. Jem had forgotten all about that injury until this moment.

He suddenly realized he'd been a fool to get himself into this fix when he wasn't at his best. But what else could he have done? Walk away and let those bullies beat up Wu Shen? Let them humiliate his friend and cut off his queue? All because Shen's family refused to give up their mine?

Another surge of fury gave Jem the strength to dodge the boys' attempts to plant his face in the dirt. A grunt from Freddy told Jem one of his kicks had hit home. But it was too little, too late. Jem was ready to cry "uncle." He hurt all over. He opened his mouth to admit defeat.

Suddenly, the pressure on his arms eased off. Tom rolled to one side and stood up.

Panting, Jem twisted around to see what had loosened Tom's grip. Will Sterling stood on the fringe, eyes bright, with his hands on his hips. *Oh, no! I'm done for. Four against one are odds nobody can beat.*

Jem and Will scuffled at least once during every school term. The rest of the year they maintained an uneasy truce. Jem saw the eager look in his eyes and knew Will would get payback today for all the times Jem had licked him in the past.

He groaned.

"You're just in time for a piece of this, Will," Dutch said, grinning. He held out the knife and nodded at Shen's long, black pigtail. "You wanna do the honors?"

Will dropped his hands to his side and ignored Dutch. Instead, he waded into the middle of the group. The smirk never left his face as he reached down and pulled Jem to his feet.

Jem tensed in readiness for the coming blows.

Then, *smack!* Will rounded on Tom and landed a punch to his mid-section. The older boy curled over and went down with a startled yelp. Dutch and Freddy gaped.

Jem took advantage of their frozen looks and yanked Shen from Dutch's grip. He gave the Chinese boy a shove that sent him reeling. "Get out of here!"

He didn't wait to see if Shen obeyed but turned to give Will a hand. He suddenly felt full of energy. He ignored his aches and pains and stepped to Will's side. Three-to-two odds were much, much better!

It looked like the bullies agreed. Tom lurched to his feet, clutching his belly. He glared at Jem and Will, but the fight had clearly gone out of him. Dutch pocketed his knife and elbowed Freddy. Without a word, the two boys scurried around the nearest corner. Tom shot one last, furious look at Jem . . . then Will . . . and slunk after his chums.

Alone with his surprising rescuer, Jem didn't know what to say. The two boys looked at each other until Will finally shrugged and turned to leave.

Jem thrust out his hand. "I don't know why you did it, but thanks just the same."

Will shook Jem's hand. "I don't know why either," he admitted. "But if the sheriff showed up, like he was bound to do if the fight went on much longer, I reckon I'd rather be on *your* side than those others."

Will dropped his hand and let out a breath. "I wish those scavengers would pack up and leave, but I've got nothin' against the China boy. Beating him up won't solve my father's or the miners' problems."

Jem looked around. "Tom and the others sure made a mess of Wu Shen's things."

Will threw up his hands and backed away. "Hold on, Jem. I helped *you*, but I'm not cleaning up after no Chinese." He turned and ran off the way he'd come.

Jem was tempted to grab Copper and gallop away. After all, he'd saved Shen's honor and helped him get away. *That's enough for one day.* His throbbing head and sore fists agreed. But Jem knew that if somebody didn't gather up the ruined laundry, Shen would return to do it. The bullies were no doubt lingering close by to have another go at him if he did.

Feeling like a fool, Jem reached down and turned the broken cart right side up. Half the town was probably looking on, but not one adult had stepped in to break up the fight.

Jem cringed. News of Pa's stand with the Chinese miners must have traveled far and fast. Nobody would be inclined to help the sheriff's son. Not today. He gathered the filthy linens and dumped them in the lopsided cart. Then he looked around for the missing wheel.

"Can I give you a hand with that?"

Jem whirled. Pa stood a few yards away, wheel in hand.

"W-why, sure, Pa," Jem stammered. He knew he looked a mess. A stay-out-of-fights-or-else scolding was surely coming his way. He reddened.

But Pa said nothing about the fight. He just quickly repaired Shen's cart and stayed close to Jem's side all the way back to Wu Jiang's laundry on China Alley.

Fight!

Aunt Rose didn't say anything about the fight either, which surprised Jem even more. Auntie was dead set against boys getting involved in scuffles of any kind. "Only low, common children resort to fists," she often said.

One look at Jem's black eye and swollen lip should have sent Aunt Rose through the roof. But she only pressed her lips together and flicked a disapproving glance at Pa, as if he had encouraged such behavior. "It appears you're more than ready to return to your ranch chores, Jeremiah," was all she said.

Pa must've pulled Auntie aside and warned her ahead of time, Jem decided two days later, sitting up on the wagon seat near the Wilsons' back door. Maybe Pa figured standing up for Wu Shen was worth getting a black eye for. Whatever the reason, Jem had gotten off scot-free from any punishment.

He waited for Nathan and Ellie to climb aboard, then released the brake and headed for Main Street.

"We just got the Morrisons' firewood to deliver," Ellie reminded him. "Then we can go out to the creek."

Jem glanced at the town's small tower clock and groaned. It read a quarter to five. Aunt Rose may not have scolded Jem for the fight, but she'd managed to fill the last two days with mountains of chores. "By the time we finish with Mr. Morrison's order, it will be too late to do any panning," he told Ellie. "But you can hop off now and go out there if you like."

A glare gave Jem his answer. Ellie had gotten a taste of her brother's firewood business last week. She clearly wanted to keep earning a few pennies stacking wood. It looked like Nathan wanted a continuing piece of the business too. For once, he was dressed for work. A pair of faded overalls had replaced the fancy duds he'd worn before.

"Hey, Jem! Wait!" A familiar voice hailed the wagon when it passed the Grand Hotel. Chad pounded into the street and snatched the horses' bridles. "Where are you off to?"

"Delivering stove wood to the mining superintendent," Jem replied.

"Need a hand?" Chad's face showed his eagerness. "I'm bored to death. Staying at the Grand is near as dull as staying out at the Sterlings."

Jem's face fell. He couldn't afford to hire any more help.

Chad laughed. "You don't need to pay me." Without waiting for an answer, he swung up on the wagon seat and squeezed in between Nathan and Ellie.

Nathan yelped and clutched the wagon seat. "Watch it! You nearly shoved me off. This seat's not big enough for four."

Jem chuckled and slapped the horses. They'd gone no more than two blocks when he pulled Copper and Silver to another stop. "Shen!" Jem called out to his friend in the street. "How are you?"

"At this rate, we'll never get done," Ellie muttered.

Jem elbowed her into silence and hopped down. One look at the cargo told Jem that Wu Shen was having a hard time today. Instead of laundry, his rickety cart was loaded down with pickaxes, shovels, drill spikes, and sledge hammers. A leather strap was wrapped around Shen's shoulders to help steady the load as he lugged it along on two wheels. Sweat beaded his forehead.

"I am fine, Jem," he said, smiling.

"Looks like you've got quite a load today."

Shen nodded. "Men bring much tools down to sharpen and repair. Must take back, make ready for new day."

"And you're dragging it clear up the hill by yourself?" Jem knew the answer. Shen always hauled things to the mine. It was his task. But Jem had never seen him with such a heavy load before, and the hill was steep.

Shen lifted the handles of his cart. "Good-bye, Jem."

"Wait," Jem said. "We're headed up to Morrisons to deliver wood. There's plenty of room for you and your tools in the back of the wagon. Hop in. We'll give you a ride."

Jem heard a muffled squeal from Ellie and hid a grin. It was no secret she was green with envy that Jem had been inside the Belle a few days ago. Nothing would please her more than to get a peek inside the old mine.

Shen hesitated then glanced up at the late afternoon sun.

"It's a hot climb up the hill in this heat," Jem remarked.

"Hotter than the inside of an oven," Ellie agreed. She was bouncing up and down on the wagon seat in her eagerness. "C'mon, Shen!"

Shen finally nodded his agreement. He untangled himself from his harness and stepped away from the cart. "I would be glad for your help."

⚔ CHAPTER 15 ⚔

The Belle Mine

Nathan, Chad, and Ellie hopped down to help Shen load the mining tools in the back of the wagon. When the last hammer had been piled in, they stashed his cart in an out-of-the-way corner off Main Street. Shen climbed into the wagon bed and settled himself between the firewood and the tools. He let out a long, weary sigh, which made Jem extra glad he'd offered his friend a lift. With all the tension in town, Shen probably dreaded walking down the street.

Copper and Quicksilver made quick work of the steep, winding road that rose just beyond Goldtown. When they passed the still-silent stamp mill, the horses veered to the right. They knew Jem's firewood route as well as he did. They looked eager to finish the route and return home to a shady pasture.

Jem clucked his tongue and directed the horses away from the Morrison place. "We've got an errand first," he told them. Copper snorted and tossed his head, but he and Silver turned and continued up the rest of the way to the Belle diggings.

The mine opening looked exactly as it had a few days before, but the same tingly thrill shot through Jem's arms at the sight. There was just something about a mine. No matter how dark and empty it appeared, there were always possibilities. A gold vein might be hiding just a few feet away, behind the rocks. One never knew.

"Oh, my!" Ellie gasped and climbed down from the wagon.

"Stay away from—" Jem paused. For once, his sister was not rushing ahead to be first. She stood with one hand clutching Copper's mane, staring at the mine entrance.

"It's lots bigger than a coyote hole," Jem said, coming up beside her. "I bet if you ask real nice, Wu Shen will let you and Nathan take a look."

Shen was all smiles. "Yes, of course. I have plenty time now."

Ellie didn't jump at the offer; which was unlike her.

"We can help you haul the tools inside," Chad offered. He looked in the wagon bed and scratched his head. "These things are heavy. We'll have to take more than one trip, unless . . ." He looked around.

Jem spied the old ore cart at the same time Chad did. It sat just outside the entrance. "Can we load the tools up in the cart and save ourselves some work?" he asked Shen.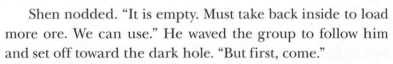

Shen nodded. "It is empty. Must take back inside to load more ore. We can use." He waved the group to follow him and set off toward the dark hole. "But first, come."

Ellie hung back.

Jem wanted to chuckle. Ellie was usually the first to plunge into an old mining hole. Of course, most of the coyote holes she and Jem explored were shallow. She'd never seen a mining hole so large—or dark-looking—before.

Shen disappeared inside the mine and hollered, "Come!"

"Maybe I'll stay with the horses," Ellie murmured.

Jem snatched her hand. "You wanted to see it, so come on."

Nathan and Chad trooped behind Jem, who held Ellie's hand as they crossed into the shadow of the Belle mine. Shen was on his knees, rummaging around inside a large wooden box. He stood up and held out a double handful of candles. "You take. Dark inside mine. Cannot see with no light." He grinned and looked proud of showing off his family's claim.

Four pairs of hands eagerly reached out. Some candles were nearly new, with plenty of use left in them. Others were stubs, good for only a few minutes of light. Jem stuffed his pockets full.

Shen brought out a small tin cylinder of matches and handed it to Jem. "Keep in pocket. Put back when we leave."

Jem was more than happy to take charge of the matches. Shen's loose-fitting tunic and pants held no pockets. If their candles went out, Jem wanted a quick way to relight them. "Can't we use the lanterns?" He glanced around for the lamps he'd seen the miners carrying the other day.

Shen shook his head. "Cannot waste kerosene."

Jem understood and nodded. "Let's get the ore cart and load up the tools."

It took three trips to unload the pickaxes, shovels, drills, and hammers from the wagon. They dropped the mining tools into the ore cart with a *clang* and began to push it.

The cart was heavier than Jem expected. They pushed and pulled it on creaking wheels into the mine. No smooth, iron tracks lined the scavenger diggings. Instead, the cart scraped and lurched its way over rusty rails on the rock-strewn tunnel floor.

They had gone no more than a stone's throw when Ellie said, "Aren't we going to light the candles?"

Jem hid a smile. Sunlight streamed in through the mine opening. They didn't need the candles yet. But he welcomed the chance to stop and rest. "You and Nathan take the lead," he told Ellie and thrust a lit candle into her hands. "Point out the holes and kick any rubble out of the way."

Step by step, they made their way through the tunnel. It was slow going. The cart creaked along, occasionally jamming up against a loose stone Nathan had missed clearing from the tracks. When that happened, Chad and Jem groaned. Only Shen plodded along, uncomplaining.

Ellie glanced back every few seconds. She looked scared. *Maybe I should have let her stay with the horses,* Jem thought. *What if she trips over one of those holes Pa warned me about?* He was opening his mouth to remind Ellie to watch where she was going, when a hand gripped his shoulder from behind.

Jem's heart leaped to his throat. He whirled. And yelled. "Hang it all, Will! What do you mean by sneaking up on me like that?"

"I didn't sneak up on you," Will yelled back. "I called, but you didn't turn around. So I followed you inside this hole." Against the bright light of the mine entrance, Will looked like a dark, inky shadow. "I was riding by and saw your wagon. What are you doing?"

None of your business. Jem's natural response to nosy Will's question came easily to his mind. But his gratitude for Will's help during the fight kept those thoughts inside where they belonged.

"We're helping Wu Shen haul mining tools." Jem kept his voice pleasant and didn't add, *What's it to you?* Instead, he said, "We could sure use another strong back to push this cart."

Will paused and looked around at the group. Then he

shrugged. "Sure. Why not? I'm here now, and"—he nodded at Jem—"I need to talk to you."

Jem frowned but said nothing. He made room for Will at the back of the ore cart and called out, "All right, let's get this thing rolling."

Ellie and Nathan held their candles up, and Chad and Shen yanked on the cart's front end. Slowly—as if it were making its final, gasping run—the ore cart began to move toward the back of the mine.

Jem didn't ask what was on Will's mind. Pushing the cart took all of his energy. But his heart beat a little faster, wondering why Will was suddenly ready to get his hands dirty.

With deep sighs and a good deal of groaning, they brought the ore cart to a halt at the end of the scavenger diggings. Candlelight flickered against the rocky sides and overhead as the boys lifted the mining tools out and piled them where Shen pointed.

"Thank you. Thank you very much," the Chinese boy said. He seemed in no hurry to shoo the boys and Ellie from his family's mine. Instead, he squatted in a corner and began organizing the tools, his face wreathed in smiles. "A fine claim, yes?"

Ellie held her candle higher. "It's . . . it's—"

"A bit gloomy," Nathan finished for her.

"More light would take care of that," Jem said. "It was bright in here the other day." He sat down on a pile of rubble to rest and looked up at Will. "What's so important that you crawled into a mine to tell me?"

Will licked his lips and waited until the rest of the group lit more candles and found places to sit. He glanced warily in Shen's direction then turned to Jem. "Father met with Judge Reece this morning."

Jem's stomach lurched. Will's tone was enough to tell Jem that the meeting had not gone well. Shen clunked around with his tools, and water dripped from the ceiling, but nobody said a word.

Will took a deep breath and continued. "The judge found a loophole in the town's mining laws." He paused.

"What kind of loophole?" Chad asked. "Spill it, Will. Don't stretch it out like you're pullin' taffy. Just get on with it."

Jem couldn't agree more. Usually, Will spread news fast and far—the unofficial town crier. Why was he holding back today? He seemed almost afraid to speak.

Will swallowed. "Foreigners can't own property, even if their claim is registered under local mining laws. Only U.S. citizens can. So"—his voice dropped—"the Chinese don't legally own this mine, no matter what the town books say."

Jem flicked a glance at Shen. The Chinese boy had finished arranging the tools. He was listening to the conversation with his head bowed. "We pay foreign miner tax each month," he whispered, looking up.

Jem nodded. "That's gotta count for something."

"I reckon it means they can mine," Will agreed, "until a citizen re-registers the claim."

"Does my pa know about this sneaky loophole?" Jem asked.

Will shook his head. "Not yet, but he'll know soon enough. Father re-registered his claim this afternoon. Judge Reece is going to tell the sheriff that he has to evict the scavengers from the Belle by tomorrow."

"*Tomorrow?*" Jem leaped to his feet. He wanted to light into Will with both fists. If the boy had acted stuck up and mean with his news, Jem would have. But Will sounded regretful, as if he knew what a hard position this court order put the sheriff in.

"Pa told Wu Hao the law is on *his* side," Jem said. "But now? If Pa has to kick them out, he'll look like just another backstabbing, Chinese-hating, white sheriff. Wu Hao will never understand."

Jem knew Pa would be furious at this legal trickery. Most likely, he would refuse to follow the judge's order. He'd lose his job as sheriff if that happened. But when it came to his principles, Pa never wavered. Jem could hear him now: "It might be *legal*, Judge, but it's not *right*. Not by a long shot."

Jem whirled on Chad, grasping for any straw of an idea. "Your pa's part owner of the Midas. Can't he do anything about this?"

"When Father finds out what Mr. Sterling has done, he'll be just as upset as your pa," Chad replied. "He's a real stickler for honor and individuals' rights—no matter what color people are." He shrugged. "But Father only owns forty percent of the Midas mine."

"What does that mean?" Ellie asked. She'd been quiet a long time.

"You should have learned your arithmetic better last term," Jem said. "It means the Carters don't own as much of the Midas as Will's family, so—"

"So Father can't overrule Mr. Sterling's decision," Chad said. "And he sure can't stop him from re-registering his claim to *this* mine." He picked up a rock and hurled it down the dark tunnel. "I wish we didn't own *any* mines." He glared at Will in the dim candlelight. "Mother wanted me to learn about the mining business, but all I've learned so far is that I'm glad I'm a rancher."

"Jem," Will said. He looked as glum as a cold fried egg. "I'm sorry too."

"Why are *you* sorry?" Jem snapped. "So what if my pa loses his job by sticking to his principles. Somebody else will force Wu Shen's family out . . . *legally*." He turned and faced the rocky wall. "I'd rather the town just shriveled up and died."

Jem was glad for the murky light and dark shadows. Tears

pricked the inside of his eyelids, and he blinked hard. *Pa lose his sheriff's job? No!* A month or two ago, Jem would have rejoiced. But not now. And certainly not in this way.

"I don't know why I care," Will said. "Maybe I've watched—and learned—a few things these past couple weeks. Ugly things. Listen, Jem. I didn't come looking for you just to spread bad news. I came to tell you how to get your pa out of this fix."

What? Jem brushed a shirt sleeve across his face and turned around. Will's eyes glinted with sudden excitement. Jem snorted. Will was a sneaky weasel and not worthy of trust. "*You're* going to figure out how to get my pa out of evicting Wu Hao without losing his job?"

Will's head bobbed up and down. He didn't seem to catch Jem's mocking tone. "I'm not going to figure it out," he said. "I've *already* figured it out."

Jem paused. For once, Will did not look like a sneak. He looked like a boy eager to share an idea to help somebody else. Did Will really have an idea? *I reckon it can't hurt to hear him out.*

"All right." Jem sat down and crossed his arms. "I'm all ears."

⚞ CHAPTER 16 ⚟

Will's Big Plan

Will plopped down next to Jem. Before he could speak, however, Nathan, Chad, and Ellie crowded around. Only Shen remained outside the group. He arranged the last of the mining tools and began to examine the rocks in one of the piles.

"Don't you want to hear this, Shen?" Ellie asked.

Wu Shen's answer was an indifferent shrug.

Jem hid a smile. His friend's ears would miss nothing, even from where he squatted next to a heaping mound of ore. Jem lit another candle, dripped wax on the ground, and jammed the lighted candle into the melted wax.

"Any way you look at it," Will began, "these scavenger diggings will go back to my father. Right or wrong, the only thing Judge Reece cares about is the law. In fact, it's already Father's claim again."

"That's just downright—"

"Oh, hush, Ellie!" Jem cut her off and scowled at Will. "You told us that already."

Will scratched his chin. He looked pleased to be the center of attention, even if it meant sitting on the ground in a dark, gloomy mine. "The Chinese miners will be driven out.

Nobody—not even your pa—can prevent it any more than he can keep the sun from rising."

Jem nodded glumly and flicked a glance at Shen. *I wonder what he thinks of this.*

"But . . ." Will lowered his voice; four heads drew closer. "If the mine were to collapse, it would be useless to the Chinese. They mine by hand. They couldn't clear the rubble enough to make these diggings ever pay again. They would move on."

"But—"

Will waved Jem quiet and kept talking. "The Midas crew has plenty of equipment, blasting powder, mules, and men to clear out this little mine in a jiffy. It could be used for the air shaft, like Father and Mr. Carter have wanted all along." Will smiled and sat back on his heels. "The mine collapses, the Chinese move on, and your father doesn't have to evict anybody."

For a full minute, nobody spoke. The air felt thick with questions, but Jem asked only one. "And just how does the Belle collapse? It's stood for years and years." He pointed up. "It's solid rock, not shored up with beams." He remembered pieces of the ceiling had broken loose the other day, but only after weeks of hammering at it. Right now, it appeared mighty sturdy.

Will rose and jammed his hands into both pockets. "With these." Slowly, he withdrew two skinny, tube-like pouches. A string hung from one end of each cloth wrapping.

Jem and the others stood and surrounded Will. Nathan brought his candle closer to give more light, but Will jerked his hands away. "Keep that candle away from this stuff!"

"What is it?" Jem asked.

"Black powder." He shrugged. "Gunpowder. It's wrapped up tight so it can be stuffed into drill holes when the miners need to blast."

"*Gunpowder?*" Jem often helped Pa load his pistols with

tiny amounts of the black granules. But he'd never seen anybody carry the stuff around in their pockets!

Will took a few steps toward the entrance and found an opening between the rocks. Then he jammed the cloth-wrapped tube into a deep crack near the ceiling and stepped back. "I've watched the Midas miners use black powder to blast new tunnels." He reached across the tunnel and found another crack. "Even a small explosion would drop enough debris in the mine to make it useless to scavengers."

"You're crazy," Chad whispered. In the smoldering candlelight, his tanned face looked like chalk. "Father uses black powder to get rid of stumps. There's no such thing as a *small* explosion."

"The little tubes control the size of the blast," Will insisted. "This can work, Jem. The Chinese *will* be evicted. The judge said so. This keeps your pa from having to be the one who does it."

Jem looked from Will to Chad then back at Will. His heart skipped a beat when he realized what Will was doing. He was reaching out to Jem, trying to make peace between them and be a friend. Will looked proud of his idea to help Jem's father.

"There's plenty of time to get out once I light the fuses," Will said. He walked back to where Jem had left his candle burning on the ground and picked it up.

Just then, Shen joined the group. He had not spoken the entire time. Now he did, but his words were few. "Very bad idea." Holding his stubby candle high, he turned his back on the others and hurried through the tunnel toward the entrance.

Jem was forced to agree with Shen. No matter how much he wanted to help Pa, he knew it was his father's decision to evict or not evict the scavenger miners. He could trust him to make the right decision. Pa did not need Jem's help. Or Will's. Especially not *this* kind of help.

Jem saw Ellie and Nathan standing close by. The reckless branding incident suddenly popped into his head. Had he learned his lesson yet? *I'm responsible for Ellie and Nathan. This is too dangerous.*

"Thanks, Will," Jem said. "I appreciate what you're trying to do. You've been a real friend today. But Pa will skin the hide offa me if I go along with this." He reached out and clasped Ellie's hand. "We've seen enough of the inside of a mine. Let's go home."

Jem didn't wait to see if Will would join them. He took Ellie's candle and held it up to light their way out.

"I'm mighty glad you didn't go along with that fool notion of Will's," Chad said when they'd gone a few steps.

Chad's words and ready smile made Jem feel good all over.

Suddenly, running footsteps echoed from the tunnel. Jem glanced behind his shoulder. The look on Will's face turned Jem's blood to ice.

"Run!" Will shouted. "I lit the—"

Ka-boom!

Blackness. Blackness so dark it numbed Jem's mind.

And dust. Thick, choking dust that made his breath come in shallow, rapid gasps.

Jem's first thought was that he'd died and gone to that place of "outer darkness," where there was "weeping and gnashing of teeth." He could understand the gnashing part. Gritty dirt filled his mouth and grated against his teeth. He tried to create enough spit to clear it, but it was no use. His tongue was drier than dust.

Jem rubbed his eyes and peered into the blackness, but it was as if someone had tied a blindfold tightly around his eyes. *No,* he corrected, *worse than a blindfold.* With a blindfold, one could often see a hint of gray, or maybe even a crack of light.

Here, there was nothing.

Jem tried to sit up, but something heavy lay across his legs. He kicked and thrashed at the heavy something until it groaned and fell away.

In a flash, everything came back. He wasn't stuck in eternal outer darkness but in the belly of a collapsed mine. He'd heard stories about trapped miners. Very few of the stories ended well. A wave of gut-wrenching fear set Jem's heart racing out of control. He squeezed his eyes shut. *Whatever else happens, God, don't let me panic. Even if I'm so scared I'm shaking, keep me brave for Ellie and Nathan. Keep me calm.*

Slowly, Jem sat up. He hurt all over, but no searing pain ripped through his arms or legs; nothing seemed broken. He ignored the ache in his head and strained to see through the dark. *The mine entrance must be somewhere.* Surely, he could find a glimmer of light from the outside world. It was still afternoon. Or was it? Jem had no idea how long he'd been unconscious.

He listened, barely breathing. The usual *drip, drip, drip* of groundwater had changed to a faint splashing. Rocks continued to settle, clunking or rolling to the ground. Jem listened harder, but he heard nothing more. No moaning or weeping; no breathing noises. Nothing.

Anger at Will's stupidity for getting them all trapped suddenly energized Jem. Blood rushed through his veins, warming his face and making his head pound. "Ellie!" he shouted. "Nathan! Chad! *Anybody!*"

His voice echoed back, unanswered. *Please, God,* Jem pleaded, *don't let them be dead.* He reached out in the direction he'd kicked the groaning something earlier and touched warm flesh. Moving his hands up and down the still body, he knew it was one of the boys. A whiff of hair tonic gave away the sleeper's identity. "Nathan!" Jem shook his cousin. "Wake up."

Nathan answered with a startled cry. He gripped Jem's arm and wouldn't let go. Then he began to sob.

The "weeping" part of that Bible verse, Jem thought. "Stop it, Nathan," he ordered. "If you're alive enough to blubber, then you're not hurt too bad." He tried to make his voice sound light and reassuring. "*Do* you hurt anywhere?"

Nathan sniffed, and his sobs lessened. "All over. But m-mostly . . . my head." He coughed. "What happened? Why is it so dark?"

"Take a—" Jem bit back his answer to such dumb questions. He remembered how confused and disoriented *he* had felt when he first came to. "Will set off the powder, and everything came tumbling down."

"C-can't you l-light a c-candle?" Nathan stammered. "It's awful dark."

Jem paused. *Why didn't I think of that? I guess my mind is still fuzzy.* He reached into his pocket and curled his fingers around two candles and the small metal tin of matches. From his other pocket, he drew out three more candles.

For the first time since the accident, Jem found himself smiling. This was something he could do, something that would keep his mind off the fact that they were trapped. Alone. In the dark. With no chance of—*stop it!*

"Good idea," he told Nathan, shoving the candles toward his cousin's voice. Fingers fumbling in the dark, Jem pulled off the top of the tin and carefully withdrew one of the precious matches. He replaced the lid and stuffed it back in his pocket. Then he scraped the match across a large rock near his boot.

The match burst into light that made Jem blink and gasp. The smell of sulfur exploded in his nostrils. A few inches away, Nathan clutched the candles and gaped at the small, bright flame. His face was black with grime. Blood had turned his pale hair rusty red. "Hurry," Nathan said, "before the match goes out."

Jem lit the candles then blew out the match. Globs of melted wax on the tunnel floor kept three of the candles in place. Nathan and Jem held the other two. Jem did not light any more, even though Nathan offered the ones in his pockets. "We should save them," he said. "It might be awhile before Pa and the rest of the town can dig us out." *If they even know where we are.*

Jem did not share this bleak thought with his cousin.

The flickering candles made the tunnel look almost cheery. "At least nobody else will have to wake up in outer darkness," Jem said. He looked around for the others, heart thudding. "Ellie!" he whispered and hurried to her side.

Ellie lay sprawled near an overhang along the side of the tunnel. The narrow outcropping had kept the larger rocks away; she was covered with only a spattering of small gravel.

Jem knelt down next to her and brushed the rubble from her hair and clothes. "Wake up," he said gently. He handed Nathan his candle and pulled Ellie into his lap. "Please wake up," he pleaded. Jem had taken his little sister into the mine. If anything happened to her because of his decision, he'd never forgive himself.

Ellie bolted upright and threw her hands over her head. "The rocks are falling!" she shrieked. Then she saw Jem and grabbed him around his neck, hugging him tight. "I wanna go home," she sobbed. "I don't like coyote holes this big."

A bubble of laugher burst from Jem's throat. Ellie was fine, completely uninjured. *Thank you, God!* "Neither do I," he told her. "Now, let go of me so we can see if Chad and Will are all right."

They found Chad half buried under some larger rocks.

Jem and Nathan freed him and shook him awake. Chad cried out in pain and sat up. "It feels like a knife is stabbing my shoulder," he rasped. "I think it got wrenched out of the socket." He took a deep, shuddering breath and clutched his left arm to keep it still. "I hurt bad."

"Don't worry," Jem told him. "Soon as we get out of here, Doc Martin will pop that shoulder right back where it belongs."

Chad gave Jem a weak smile then leaned his head back against the tunnel wall and closed his eyes. "If I keep still, I can stand it."

Jem glanced around for Will and saw he was already awake. He appeared uninjured, huddled next to the rock wall, with his knees pulled up under his chin. His eyes were wide and scared-looking. Tears ran down his cheeks, leaving muddy trails. His breath came in choking gulps. "I'm sorry . . . I'm sorry," he moaned. "It wasn't supposed to happen this way."

Jem squatted beside him. "Oh? How is a mine explosion *supposed* to happen, Will?" He was so angry, he wanted to shake him. Blowing things up with gunpowder was danger-ous and unpredictable. Of *course* it wouldn't turn out the way Will planned.

Jem was only spouting off, covering up his own terror with surly words. But Will looked up and answered as if Jem really wanted to know. "The mine was supposed to come down *behind* us. You know, where I set the powder in the cracks. Way back there." He pointed toward the shadows. A pile of debris partially blocked the tunnel. "Then we could just run out through the mine entrance."

"It looks like the explosion blew up more than just one part of this old mine," Jem said. "It's a miracle more of the ceiling didn't fall on us." He stood up, held his candle high, and started toward the entrance.

"Don't leave, Jem," Ellie whimpered. She stumbled over to her brother and grasped his hand. "Take me with you."

Ellie's hand was ice-cold. Jem squeezed it, then gently peeled her fingers away. "I'm not going far," he said. "I want to see how much of the tunnel is blocked. Stay with Nathan. I'll be right back."

Ellie dropped her hand to her side and stepped aside without an argument. Jem should have been pleased. Holding Ellie back was usually a full-time job. But from the moment Jem had led her into the Belle mine, his sister's spunk had fizzled away. *She changed her mind about seeing this hole, but I dragged her in here anyway.*

Cautiously, Jem picked his way around piles of rocks, some the size of small boulders. He heard a low rumbling then a large *crack*. Jem dodged a shower of fist-sized stones that tumbled to the ground in front of him. Waving away the dust, he took a few more steps and came face to face with a mound of rubble that filled the tunnel from top to bottom.

A feeling of panic rose at the sight of the blocked tunnel. Jem clenched his jaw and swallowed his alarm. *This is really bad, God. But I know You're here. You must have a way out for us. Or a way in for Pa. I have to trust You and stay calm.*

"Jem!" Ellie's frightened shout bounced off the tunnel walls. "What was that noise?"

"Just a little rock shower," he yelled back. "I'm fine."

Jem wasn't fine. Not really. He couldn't keep his hands from shaking. The candlelight wobbled all over the place. He hurried back to the group and sat down. "The way out is completely blocked." He let out a long, dismal breath. "But I knew that before I checked. There wasn't a glimmer of light when I woke up. Not from anywhere."

A choked cry burst from Will. His face turned white. "That means"—he gulped—"that means I've killed Wu Shen." He buried his head in his knees and sobbed.

⊰ CHAPTER 17 ⊱

No Way Out

Jem sucked in his breath at Will's words. *Wu Shen!* The Chinese boy had run ahead, no doubt in a hurry to get away from crazy Will Sterling and his black powder. How far had Shen gone before the explosion? "Maybe he got out in time," Jem said weakly. He slumped to the tunnel floor.

Will shook his head. "He's buried under a pile of rocks. I know he is. He's dead."

Ellie started crying. "Are we gonna die too?"

"Probably," Will said. His voice rose higher. "We're trapped. We'll never get out. I deserve to die. I killed—"

"Shut up!" Chad roused long enough to shout.

Jem dropped his candle and lunged for Will. He grabbed him by the shoulders. "Don't you scare my sister, or I'll slap you silly. What's the matter with you?" He whirled on Ellie. "Quit blubbering. Nobody's going to die." He shouted the words, hoping to convince himself it was true.

The fate of other trapped miners came to mind, but he pushed those stories into a little-used corner of his memory. "It's just going to be a long night," he finished.

"That's for sure," Nathan muttered. He picked up the dropped candle and touched the wick to his own candle's flame. Then he handed it to Ellie. "Here. Hold Jem's candle. Maybe it'll perk you up."

Jem knew better. One little candle was not going to perk Ellie up. Not now. Not with Will spouting fools' talk about dying. But he gave Nathan a grateful nod. With Chad in so much pain he could barely talk, and Will ready to jump over the edge of a hysterical cliff, Jem was glad he could count on his cousin. Perhaps he and Nathan could hold things together for the others.

Pale but determined-looking, Nathan nodded back.

"Ellie," Jem said, using his you-better-mind-me-or-else voice, "I want you to keep Chad company. He's hurt. He needs somebody to look after him."

Ellie's tears dried up. She gripped her candle tighter, flicked a glance at Chad, and nodded.

Jem smiled. Tending hurt animals always sparked Ellie's interest, even if she was only rescuing a baby chick and returning it to its mother. Chad was no baby chick, and he probably didn't care if Ellie sat by him or not. His eyes were closed, and his face showed a peculiar shade of gray under the dirt.

But it will keep Ellie busy and her mind off dying. It won't hurt Chad any, either. Jem gave himself a mental pat on the back for taking care of one problem. If only the rest of their problems could be solved so easily!

When the first of their candles sputtered and died, Jem's feelings of accomplishment drained away. A puddle of melted wax was all that remained of the candle stump he'd jammed into the mess . . . how long ago? Jem had lost track of the time. He wished he had one of those fancy watches with a chain, like the mayor carried around in his vest pocket.

Jem and Nathan exchanged grim looks. He knew what his cousin was thinking. It was going to get mighty dark in a hurry. Nathan emptied his pockets and piled five more candles on the ground. Without a word, he hurried over to Chad.

While Nathan knelt and carefully fished around in Chad's pockets for the precious light sources, Jem stood over Will. "I don't suppose you brought any candles along with your black powder."

Will gave a muffled "No" and went back to rocking and sniveling. "Go away."

For a long minute, Jem looked down at Will and listened to his muttering. Most of the boy's words were jumbled and confused, but "God is punishing me for sure" came out loud and clear. Will sounded close to his limit. Any moment, he might snap and do something crazy, like the miner in one of Strike's prospecting stories.

He'd told Jem that he and a dozen others had once been trapped for nine days in absolute darkness. They were so cold, they tied bandanas around their heads and chins to keep their teeth from chattering. On the ninth day, they heard a sudden shriek, then gibberish. Then the sound of running feet, a body falling, and more running. Then silence. Strike said a miner's mind had snapped. When rescue came, they were all saved but the one who had run off.

Listening to Will's ramblings, Jem felt his stomach tie in knots. It would be so easy to give in, so easy to let fear take over and turn him into a quivering blob of flesh—just like Will and that other miner. But deep inside, Jem knew things weren't as bad as the picture Will was painting in his guilty, terror-stricken mind. They had escaped the worst of the cave-in. In fact . . .

Jem squatted beside Will and laid a hand on his arm. "Simmer down, Will. You're working yourself up for no reason. God's not punishing you or anybody else. Just the opposite. He put a bubble around us. We're alive. No bones broken. No crushed skulls."

Will looked at Jem with red-rimmed eyes. His nose ran freely; he didn't bother to wipe it. His arms continued to clasp his knees, and his whole body trembled. "I thought . . . I thought . . ." He paused.

Jem leaned closer and kept his voice quiet. "What did you think?"

"I thought the f-fuses were long enough to g-give us time," he stammered. "Now, we'll most l-likely suffocate down here or starve to death. Even if we do get out, Wu Shen's family will hate me. Your pa will arrest me and—"

"That's fools' talk," Jem snapped. "Haven't you got any gumption at all?" He immediately regretted lashing out. *Simmer down!* he ordered his whirling thoughts. "I'm sorry," he said aloud. Then he sighed. "You and I just can't get along, can we? Always throwing words or fists at each other."

Will shrugged and said nothing. But at least he had stopped blubbering. He pulled a handkerchief from his back pocket and blew his nose. Then he stared in the direction of the mine entrance.

Jem followed his gaze. "We're going to get out of here, Will."

Will kept staring into the dark passageway. "How do you know?"

Jem didn't know . . . not yet. He only knew that if Will didn't hear some kind of hope, he might jump clean over the edge of his mental cliff. *Please don't let him snap like that other miner,* he prayed. The thought of Will screaming like a lunatic prodded Jem to dig deep into his memory.

Then he remembered something. His heart leaped. *Thank you, God!* "I know we're going to get out of here," he said, "because of my name."

"Huh?" Will scrunched up his face in disbelief. "Your *name?*"

Nathan left the pile of candles and wandered over to

listen. From a few yards away, Ellie's chatter ceased. She sat next to Chad, but she was looking at her brother. Chad watched Jem too, glassy-eyed and clearly hurting.

Jem had everybody's attention now. *Good.* "You heard right, Will. My name's Jeremiah, like the prophet in the Bible. Pa says I need to 'gird up my loins' like my namesake and never forget that God has a plan."

Jem looked up. Dark shadows lurked in the cracks of the rocky ceiling. He shivered. "Sometimes I forget. When I do, I get scared, *really* scared. Like you, Will. But just now I remembered what the other Jeremiah wrote: 'For I know the thoughts that I think toward you,' saith the Lord," Jem recited, "'thoughts of peace, and not of evil, to give you an expected end.' So, I know God has a plan, and it's a good one."

Silence greeted Jem's words. A distant rock dropped into an unseen puddle of water with a loud *plop*. Ellie startled at the noise.

"Hear that?" Jem said. "There's plenty of water close by. The Belle mine is not very big. We just need to sit tight for a couple of days until they dig us out. Our wagon is tied up outside the mine. How can anybody not know we're in here?"

Will nodded. "That's right. My horse is there too." Color returned to his face, and he let out a long, shuddering breath. "Thoughts of peace and not evil," he whispered. "An expected end." It looked like Will was rolling the two phrases around in his frightened mind. Jem hoped the verse stuck tight and kept Will calm.

"Well," Nathan said, "if we're going to be here for a couple of days, I think we should blow out all the candles but one."

"No!" Ellie yelled, but Jem shushed her. It made sense to conserve their light.

"We light one candle at a time and stretch them out,"

Nathan went on. "Ellie can hold the candle and be the light bearer."

"But we blow it out when we go to sleep," Chad put in.

Everyone turned to look at him. Chad sat shivering, and Jem noticed for the first time how cool the air felt. A mine was a blessed relief from a sweltering summer's day, but the longer Jem stayed below ground, the less he liked the damp, chilly air.

"I'm not sleeping a wink," Ellie said, "so nobody's blowing out *my* candle." She held it away from Chad, far out of range of his breath.

Jem had to use all his wits to sweet-talk Ellie into letting her light go out. "Don't be silly. You'll fall asleep soon enough. Your candle will drop to the ground and go out anyway." Before she could protest, Jem added, "Give me your candle. You can sleep next to me. I promise I won't blow it out until you're sound asleep."

"You told me to stay with Chad."

"Fine." Jem pulled himself to his feet and joined Ellie and Chad against the far wall. "Are you thirsty? I can dump out the matches and use the little tin to get you some water."

Ellie giggled. The sound was so natural, so *Ellie*, that Jem grinned. Nathan chuckled. Even Will cracked a half-smile.

"Fetch water in that teensy thing?" She giggled again. "Now who's being silly? I can wait 'til morning—whenever *that* is—and find my own water." Then her face fell. "Anyway, you need the match tin to bring Chad water, since he hurts too much to get his own."

Jem bit his lip and looked at his friend.

"I'm fine," Chad whispered. "I'm not thirsty. But I'm tired. And cold."

"So am I," Nathan said from the other wall. He lay down in the dirt and curled up into a tight ball.

Jem took the candle from Ellie and motioned her to lie

down. She propped her head in Jem's lap and—in spite of her promise not to sleep a wink—was snoring softly in less than five minutes. Soon, Nathan and Chad were out cold. Chad sat against the wall, with his head thrown back and his mouth hanging open. Only Will and Jem remained awake.

Jem wanted to wait until everyone fell asleep before he plunged the mine into "outer darkness." Will, especially, might panic. "Aren't you tired?" Jem asked, yawning.

Will nodded. "But before you blow out the candle, I was wondering if . . ." His voice trailed off.

"Wondering what?" Jem prompted.

"If you know any more verses from Jeremiah," Will whispered. "The prophet you're named for."

Jem nodded. "There's lots of verses in Jeremiah I like."

"No wonder you always win the Sunday school Bible verse contest," Will muttered.

Jem ignored Will's remark. "I know a good verse. It's 'Call unto me, and I will answer thee, and shew thee great and mighty things.' I'm thinkin' it might be a good idea to call on God and ask Him to show us a way out of here."

Will brightened. "I will if you will."

After a quick prayer, Jem blew out the candle. For some reason, the absolute darkness did not feel as black as it had before. A warm presence seemed to surround Jem. He stopped shivering and let sleep take him away.

⊰ CHAPTER 18 ⊱

The Price of a Mine

Jem jerked awake, shivering uncontrollably. Any feeling of warmth had long since vanished. His teeth chattered, and his fingers felt like chunks of ice. He sat up and discovered that his arms, legs, and backside were soaked. Water dripped from his sleeves. He clamped his hands under his armpits and clenched his jaw to keep his teeth still.

What happened? What's wrong? His mind was as chilled as the rest of his body. And no wonder. He was sitting in water a few inches deep. Hands shaking, Jem fished in his pocket for the tin of matches. He opened it and struck one against the rock wall. Nothing happened. It took three tries before one of the matches sputtered to life.

Jem looked around. A shiny expanse of water covered half the tunnel floor. Slowly but steadily, the seeping ground water was rising. He remembered the small, bubbling stream outside the mine. The explosion must have given the water a new place to go. *This is bad!*

The light went out, and the rest of the matches were waterlogged and useless. Jem's heart sank. He couldn't see clearly. Chad, Nathan, and Will were gray forms pressed up against the rocky sides of the mine. Ellie was a dark shadow lying next to him.

Then he gasped. *I can see them!* Jem leaped to his feet. "Wake up, everybody! I see light!"

Hope surged like a fire through Jem, warming his arms and legs. He splashed through the shallow water until he came to a shaft of daylight shining down from above. Part of the ceiling near where the tunnel was blocked had completely caved in. To Jem, it looked like a light from heaven.

He whooped. "It's a hole. I see daylight."

"Is it big enough to crawl through?" Nathan asked, clomping his way to Jem's side.

Will joined the boys and glanced up. "God showed us, just like you prayed," he said in a hushed voice. He stared at Jem. "Can we get out?"

Jem nodded. "It's not too far up. Somebody could stand on my shoulders and reach the surface. But . . ."

"But what?" Will demanded.

"You and Nathan are too heavy to shove through that hole," Jem said.

Will's face fell.

Jem grinned. "Don't worry. I know somebody who's just right for this job."

Two minutes later, Ellie stood under the hole in the mine ceiling. She wrapped her arms around her body and shivered, looking up with wide, hazel eyes.

"Well? Can you do it?" Jem asked. "Can you squeeze through that hole and go for help? You just need to run down to the mine entrance and bring Pa and the others here."

"What if n-nobody's there?" Ellie said between chattering teeth.

"They are," Jem assured her. "But if they're not, then—"

"Then you can ride my horse and go find them," Will offered.

Ellie whirled on Will. "Ride Prince Charming?" A grin split her face. "I'll do it." But when she learned *how* she would

135

have to climb through the hole, she changed her mind. "I have to stand on your shoulders?" She shook her head. "No, Jem."

"Why not?"

Ellie crossed her arms and scowled. "Because"—her face reddened—"you'll see under my dress, and that's not proper."

Nathan gave a choked laugh, and Will rolled his eyes. From the tunnel, out of sight in the shadows, Chad snickered.

Jem slapped a hand against his forehead. "Roasted rattle-snakes, Ellie! I've seen your bloomers a hundred times."

"Especially right after Mother made them," Nathan added. "You twirled all over the house in those silly things."

Ellie narrowed her eyes. "What about *him*?" She unfolded her arms and jabbed a finger at Will. "He might see and tell Maybelle."

Will shook his head. "She's the last person I'd tell anything to. But if it makes you happy, I'll sit with Chad. Just go get help!" Muttering, he left the shaft of light, leaving Jem, Nathan, and Ellie alone.

Jem started laughing. It was a miracle what hope did for a person. Will was acting like his old self, and Ellie was being a bother. They'd even gotten a chuckle out of Chad.

With Nathan's help, Ellie soon stood on her brother's shoulders. She reached up through the rocky ceiling to balance herself and squealed. "I can feel the dirt and see the trees. It's nice and warm up here. Push me higher."

Jem and Nathan took hold of Ellie's high-topped shoes and lifted her as high as they could reach. There were a few groans, an "ouch!" and suddenly their hands were empty.

Ellie poked her head back through the opening and yelled, "I'll be right back!"

"It's been hours," Will whined.

It did seem like hours, but Jem didn't say anything. He, Nathan, and Will sat below the opening, waiting and hoping. Even Chad had summoned enough strength to move from the shadows to be near the shaft of sunlight. The seeping water had not yet reached this part of the tunnel, and there were plenty of dry spots to perch on.

Jem idly picked up a rock and tossed it down the tunnel. It *plopped* in the water. He threw another. Soon, Will and Nathan joined him. The *plop, plop, plip-plop* kept Jem's mind from ticking off the seconds. *What's taking Ellie so long?*

"Uh . . . fellas?" Chad interrupted Jem's rock throwing.

Jem paused. "What?"

"Maybe you should take a look at the rocks you're chucking." He pointed with his good arm. "There's a lot of sparkling dust around here. And this *is* a gold mine."

A closer glance told the story. The rocks were worthless ore, but it looked like the blast had loosened a large quantity of placer gold from the surface. It had settled on the tunnel floor and—Jem noticed—all over their clothes. The light from above set the dust to glittering.

"You're right." Jem's heart leaped, like it always did when he discovered a bit of gold. "But right now I'd trade it all to be up there." He pointed toward the patch of sky.

The next moment a shadow blocked the opening. Pa's voice called, "Stand clear. I'm coming down." A rope dropped through the hole, and Pa slid into the mine so fast that Jem thought the rope might be greased. He didn't wait for Pa to get his bearings. He slammed into him and nearly crushed him in a tight hug.

"Oh, Pa! Oh, Pa!" Jem didn't have to be brave any longer. Pa was here. He'd get them out of this fix, and he'd get Will, Nathan, and Chad out too. "What took you so long?"

Pa laughed and ruffled Jem's hair. "It's only been half

an hour. We were digging all night at the entrance, but Morrison reckoned it would be a couple more days before we broke through. Then Ellie showed up, howling like a banshee. Soon as we heard her story, we dropped everything, grabbed some rope, and headed up here."

He smiled at the other boys. "We'll have you out of here in no time." His gaze fell on Chad. "Ellie says you're hurt. Your pa went for the doctor."

"Yes, sir," Chad said. "It's my shoulder. Popped right out and hurts awful bad."

"We'll lower Doc Martin into this hole to fix you up." Pa grinned. "Most unusual house call he's ever made, I reckon."

Chad managed a weak smile.

Pa made short work of tying a loop in the end of the rope. "Step into the loop and hang on. The men above will do the rest." He paused. "Who wants to go first?"

In the end, Will went first. Jem wanted to stay and see how Chad made out. Besides, Pa was here now, so the collapsed mine no longer held any terrors. It was just a cold, dirty, oversized coyote hole.

"Mr. Morrison heard—or actually felt—the explosion late yesterday afternoon," Pa explained. He settled Nathan on the lifeline next and gave the signal to pull him up. "So we knew something bad had happened even before Wu Shen burst into my office screeching in Chinese."

"Wu Shen?" Jem yelled. "He's not dead? He escaped?" *Thank you, God! You rescued us, and now Will won't have to feel so guilty.*

"By the hairs of his pigtail," Pa said. "When I got him simmered down enough to speak English, he told me the whole tale." He took a deep breath and let it out slowly. "Will Sterling nearly got you all killed. I've a good mind to—"

"No, Pa," Jem broke in, shaking his head. "Will just

138

wanted to help you. And me. He knows what he did. I . . . I think he's been punished enough."

Pa's eyebrows shot up. For a minute he was quiet. "Will's father has had a hard, soul-searching night as well," he finally admitted. "Digging next to him was no pleasure, let me tell you. The man was frantic to save you kids. He blames himself for the whole thing."

"Is he still going to make you evict Wu Shen's family from the claim?" Jem swallowed and waited for the answer.

Pa shook his head. "No need. Will's little ploy worked, however shameful it was." He glanced around at the rubble and sighed. "The mine is no good to Wu Hao now. The Midas will get its air shaft. But at what cost?" He pulled Jem into a warm embrace. "Thank God this air shaft didn't cost us your lives. That's what matters most."

Doc Martin was lowered into the hole a few minutes later and brought Chad much-needed relief. With his shoulder back in place and a dose of painkiller, Chad had no trouble being hauled up. "I'm gonna stick to chasing cattle," he joked as he rose toward daylight. "I've had me a bellyful of gold mines."

Jem agreed. He never wanted to see the inside of a mine again.

It was soon his turn to grab the rope. Jem emerged from the Belle diggings and into the bright noon light, blinking hard. He lifted his face to the sun, closed his eyes, and soaked in its blistering rays. "I will never complain about the heat again," he said with a long, relieved sigh.

Well-wishers surrounded him; very few eyes remained dry. In a mining camp like Goldtown, everyone knew the horror of loved ones trapped underground—and the relief that came when they were brought out alive.

Jem suddenly felt himself engulfed in a bear hug. He opened his eyes to see Strike-it-rich Sam holding him in a tight, one-armed grip. Tears glistened in the prospector's eyes. "Heard about the accident. They wouldn't let me dig, but I was givin' the Good Lord an earful the whole time. Glad to see you're still with us, boy." He let Jem go and wiped his brow. "That was pert-near the longest night of my life."

"Mine too," Jem agreed. He glanced around. "Say, have you seen Wu Shen? I—" His eyes widened. Spread out on the hillside above the mine, dozens of men were scooping dirt from the forested ground into wheelbarrows and gunny-sacks. "What's going on?"

"Appears you young'uns started a minor gold strike here-abouts. The Sterling boy came outta that hole all covered in sparkly dirt. Didn't take long for word to spread." He chuckled. "It won't last, on account of it's just surface gold, but it'll keep folks busy while they're waitin' for the Midas to reopen." Strike laughed louder. "Sterling ain't sayin' a word about the miners crawlin' all over his claim. Reckon he's had a change o' heart."

Jem grinned. It was good to see the miners scratching away at the topsoil—just like during Goldtown's boom days. Then he spotted a small figure sitting under a tree and waved good-bye to Strike.

Wu Shen's face brightened when Jem ran up and fell to the ground beside him. "We thought you were dead!" Jem said with a gasp. "Caught in the falling debris. Will went a little crazy, thinkin' he killed you."

"Yes," Shen said. "He find me and say he very sorry."

"He did?" It appeared that a night in a collapsed mine had changed Will for the better. "I'm glad you're all right, Shen, but it's too bad about your folks' mine. What will they do now?"

Shen gave Jem a sly grin. "Sheriff say Sterling must pay for claim. Much, *much* money. And my father say he will leave and work on new railroad. He not go before because of claim." He cocked his head, looking puzzled. "I do not believe a track can stretch from east to west. But Father say pay is good to cut through mountains. Many Chinese go. It is honorable work." He shrugged. "Maybe they make this trans-con-ti-nen-tal railroad happen."

"Will you go?" Jem asked. He hoped Shen would not join the venture. It sounded dangerous, blasting through mountains.

Shen shook his head. "Uncle Jiang need me to help with laundry." He laughed. "Maybe I start best Chinese laundry in California."

Jem laughed along with his friend. "I sure could use a Chinese laundry right now. These clothes are filthy." He looked down. Mixed in with the dirt and grime, gold dust speckled his shirt and britches. A *lot* of gold dust. He must have picked up more coming through the hole—his own little "stake" of the new gold strike.

"On second thought," he told Shen, "I think I'll do my own laundry today." He grinned. "I've got some gold to wash."

Historical Note

When prospectors first arrived in the California gold fields in 1849, they found gold scattered along riverbeds or buried just below the surface of the ground as dust, flakes, or nuggets. These forms of gold were called "placer deposits." It was easy to separate placer gold from dirt with a shovel, a gold pan, and a source of running water.

It wasn't long, however, before the placer gold began to disappear. The only gold left was buried deep under the earth in deposits called "lodes" or "veins." The gold was embedded in quartz rock, called "ore," and ran in all directions underground. The trick was to figure out where a gold vein was located. Miners dug shafts in places where placer gold had been found earlier. This was called "hard-rock" mining, and it was backbreaking work. Many times the miner was rewarded with only an empty hole.

When digging by hand became too difficult, teams of men with machinery and explosives took over. A company was formed and went to work. Miners labored underground all day (or all night), drilling, blasting, shoveling, and hauling the ore to the surface. Mining was dangerous work, especially extending the tunnels.

Miners known as "blasters" created explosives by filling paper tubes with black powder and inserting a long fuse.

142

(Dynamite came along much later.) They stuffed the explosive in a drilled hole and shouted "Fire in the hole!" Then they ran like mad. Each blast could extend a tunnel by three feet.

Mules brought the ore carts to the surface, where the gold-bearing rock was crushed in the stamp mill. The stamps were sets of iron rods with heavy, metal weights on the ends. The stamps were lifted and dropped on the ore, pounding it into fine sand. The noise was deafening.

Once the gold ore became fine particles, the gold could be separated from the worthless rock. Poisonous chemicals like mercury (quicksilver) were used to draw the gold out. After the gold was separated, it was poured into molds, where it cooled and hardened into gold bars.

Visit www.GoldtownAdventures.com to download a free literature guide with enrichment activities for *Tunnel of Gold*.

About the Author

Susan K. Marlow is a twenty-year homeschooling veteran and the author of the Circle C Adventures and Circle C Beginnings series. She believes the best part about writing historical adventure is tramping around the actual sites. Although Susan owns a real gold pan, it hasn't seen much action. Panning for gold is a *lot* of hard work. She prefers to combine her love of teaching and her passion for writing by leading writing workshops and speaking at young author events.

You can contact Susan at susankmarlow@kregel.com.